EMISSARY OF VENGEANCE

A Lucas Martell Novel, Book 2

WILLIAM JACK STEPHENS

Sterling Adventure Group, LLC

THE LUCAS MARTELL SERIES

Mallorca Vendetta

Emissary of Vengeance

Merchant of Souls
(To be released in Spring 2020.)

Everyone on my mailing list will receive advanced notice!

Get connected with me here: **Mailing List Sign Up**

Or at my website: www.williamjackstephens.com

I

PUNTO MATANZAS, CUBA

When the moon is in the final nights of waxing to full, you can actually feel the tide preparing to turn. Most particularly in the months of summer, when the air is hot and moist, and the moon rises after midnight. The sparkling blackness of the Caribbean Sea is indistinguishable from the starry sky, until the moon parts them on the horizon, then balances briefly on the waterline. The sea draws a deep breath, then slowly releases, and the waves turn to face the shore.

The tide was turning now on a little inlet beach in the mangrove flats of eastern Cuba. Turning as well for the future of Paulo, the young man stripped, stretched, and tied among the mangrove roots. He had been put there at the lowest ebb, when the roots are fully exposed like charcoaled teepee poles embedded in the mud, and the bushy green leaves perched in the air above. Paulo's death was going to take some time.

He hadn't done anything terribly bad, nor offended anyone that he could remember. His only sin was loyalty for a man he had never met. A man who was likely as evil as the ones who were doing this to poor little Paulo. But since the age of thirteen, the man he had never known had kept him safe, kept his family well fed, and made him part of a much larger family. A cartel family that stretched far beyond the sea around Cuba, to the nations south and north, east and west.

Paulo refused to give up any information about this man he worked for, and for this, he was going to die. He was staring up through the mangrove roots at the constellation Orion, and silently praying for his soul.

One of the two men overseeing his slow demise, spoke, "It might take an hour for the water to come in over your face, Paulo, but the crabs will come back to the shore ahead of the tide. You know, those nasty little red and yellow bastards. They have a fondness for blood."

After staking Paulo out in the mucky sand below the mangroves, the men had made small incisions in the soft tissue of his inner thighs with a knife, precariously near his groin. The sweet blood was dribbling down and pooling in the sand.

The man rotated his wrist to glance at the

luminescent hands of his watch. The second man said something in Russian, and they both laughed.

The first man was Cuban. Barefoot, wearing dark slacks that were rolled above his knees to keep them from getting wet. The only thing visible in the darkness was his perfectly pressed, white short sleeved shirt that reflected an amber color in the moonlight. He pulled a cigar from his pocket, clipped the end, and placed it in his mouth, gently rolling it in his lips to dampen the long wrapped outer leaf. He struck a match, and the pulsing flame revealed his tanned face and oily black hair as he sucked the fire deeply into the end of the cigar three times.

He walked over and stood looking down at Paulo, "My comrade thinks you are too stupid to save yourself."

Looking up, Paulo could only see the black halo of the man's face behind the orange glow of the cigar, "I'm smart enough to know that no one can save me," he said.

"I've told you many times, if you just tell me who you work for, and how I can find him, then I will let you go. You don't have to die."

"I'm not afraid to die. I won't tell you anything!"

The tip of the cigar flared as the dark haired man drew hard and held it for just an instant. He lightly popped his lips in a round shape, and the thick, sickly bluish smoke drifted down over Paulo's face.

"It won't just be you who dies, Paulo. If I don't

leave here with the information I need, then I'll find your wife and ask her. She's a pretty girl, Paulo, and you have a baby now too, yes?"

Paulo's expression suddenly changed, though it could barely be seen in the moonlight. The lines across his forehead clenched. He hesitated, then said, "If I tell you anything, they will kill my whole family!"

"I'm going to kill them if you don't. You should worry about the man in front of you, Paulo. Not the ones who are not here." He looked at his watch once again, "The water is rising Paulo. Tell me what you know, and I promise that your family will be safe. This island belongs to us, and no one will harm them. Tell me now, Paulo, who are you working for? Is he a Mexican? A Columbian? What's the name of the cartel?"

Paulo began to sob. He sputtered, then blurted out, "I don't know his real name. They always just called him 'El Carnicero', *The Butcher.*"

"And where is El Carnicero from? Is he part of a cartel? They've been shipping opioids and counterfeit drugs from China through the Caribbean, Paulo. Taking food from the mouths of all of us and our children. Tell me Paulo, and you won't suffer a moment longer."

Paulo burst into more tears, "The Sun," he cried.

"What?" the man asked, as if he couldn't have heard correctly.

"The Sun. They are the men of the sun."

. . .

THE DARK MAN and his Russian-speaking comrade stepped away from the sandy beach as the water inched forward, and they turned and walked along a narrow path through the mangroves, up to a gravel road where a black van was parked.

"Is this going to be a problem?" the Russian asked.

"No. In fact, it might work to our advantage," the dark haired man said. "I haven't heard that name in several years, but I know exactly who he is talking about." His face glowed in the orange light as he drew again on the cigar. Then they heard the first screams echoing up from the beach. They looked at each other and laughed again.

"I believe the little crabs have found the meal we left for them," the Russian said.

❧ 2 ❧

SEVILLE, SPAIN

Seville, Spain was not what he had imagined. He expected orchards that covered the rolling dry hills, and white colonial mansions with mustard-colored window trim and tall oak doors. There would be wine tastings in the cool evenings on a stone terrace with attractive young women. That is what he had envisioned in his mind.

His new mentor had suggested the month in Seville. Said he knew a man who could bring his skills up to par for the new line of work to which Lucas Martell had recently devoted himself. Skills that, for the lack of, nearly cost him his life just a few months earlier when he faced a Moroccan wielding a rusty knife. Lucas had survived, but not by much, and not without a nasty scar that still festered on damp rainy days.

And here he was, facing a new enemy who was determined to leave him with more scars.

The basement beneath the old Moorish castle was dark and musty, only a few slivers of sunlight piercing through the center of the room from the slender ground level windows. A thin cloud of dust, disturbed from the dirt floors, hung motionless at chest level in the room, and the pungent odor of old white-oak sherry barrels burned in the back of his throat.

He stood perfectly still with his back wedged in the shadow of two barrels, and subconsciously held his breath. He listened and waited for his attacker to reveal himself. He thought he heard the rustle of bare feet over sand, but saw nothing in the room move. He glimpsed a shadow swimming soundlessly across the far wall, then the slightest swirl in the gray dust in the air followed moments later.

His patience was wearing thin. He grew tired of the games his tormentor was playing with him, he stepped into the center of the room in the faint light. "Let's end this!" he shouted into the dark.

He stood crouched at the knees, his left hand held loosely in front to block an attack and his knife-hand tucked close with the long blade reversed, dagger style. The shadow made no sounds or movement. Lucas pivoted left, then back to the right, growing more impatient with each passing second.

He felt it before he ever heard it coming. The slippery slice across the tendons in the back of his knees, and he reflexively twisted his upper body and reached down to block the attack too late. He realized his mistake in the next instant, as the killing strike came over his lowered hand and slashed across his left jugular vein.

LUCAS STOOD straight and his arms fell to his sides, "I'm dead again. I'm wasting your time with this. I should just stick with firearms." Then he reached up and wiped away the grease mark left on his neck by the training blade.

His instructor, Marcelo, was a legendary Spanish blade master, raised in the knife-fighting schools of Seville, and the private tutor of many world renowned assassins.

"No, no, you've improved very much over the last month. Your technique is very good when you fight in the open and in the daylight. But there is something about the darkness that unsettles you. It's not fear, I can see that you have no fear of death. But you grow too anxious. What are You thinking about?"

Lucas had spent years as a sniper with the French Foreign Legion, stationed in the killing fields in Central Africa and the Middle East. Spent days, weeks sometimes, perched in the thorn tangles of a mountainside or sand dune, controlling the beat of his own heart and waiting patiently for a single perfect moment to pull the trigger. Never once had he been overly anxious.

Only twice had he ever lost control of his emotions. The first time, at the age of seventeen when he fought the man who was kidnapping his little sister; a dark, evil man, with a long rusty blade. The second time was when he encountered that same man, the Moroccan, in a darkened warehouse on the fishing pier in Mallorca, twelve years later, again, with knife in hand.

"It's only when a knife is involved, " he said. "I see that now. It's something old. Something I have to face."

"Well then, that's why my friend William was so insistent that I take you in for training. No worries, I'm the finest knife-fighting master in the world. You will be very proficient when you leave here."

3

DULLES AIRPORT, WASHINGTON D.C.

The tall slender man walked out of the main exit at Dulles Airport, and it felt all too familiar. He had been here many times before, either leaving for missions somewhere in the world, or returning for debriefings at CIA headquarters in Langley, just a one-hour drive east. But this time was different. This was the first time in nearly forty years that he came through Dulles with no mission purpose.

He looked past the long line of cabs parked at the curb, up to the private-car loading area, and saw a driver standing with a sign in hand, "Mr. William Diggs."

Bill Diggs had decided to come home for the first time in many years. Home, was the small farmhouse that sat on a hill, looking out over twenty-five acres of rolling emerald pasture on the edge of Winchester,

Virginia. It was the home he so desperately wanted to get away from when he was a boy, and now that both of his parents were dead, it was his. It was the only piece of property he had ever owned, or likely ever would, because his life had never been well suited to being rooted in one place.

Traveling west from Dulles felt odd, and oddly comforting at the same time. The highway through Leesburg was lined with warehouses and office complexes, where there were once forests of elms and pines. The road now went around Leesburg to avoid the city-sized traffic. But another hour farther west toward the Shenandoah Valley, the hills grew more pronounced and the evidence of growth waned. It felt more reassuringly rural.

As they entered Winchester, Diggs was surprised to see new neighborhoods, a golf course development, and life coming back to the town he had left years ago. The central street, once fallen into ruin and claimed by the homeless and bands of small-time drug dealers, was completely restored. The traffic had been diverted around, and Main Street turned into a trendy brick-paved walking route, with shops, restaurants, and holiday travelers. The little town was coming to life again, after so many years of stagnating.

Diggs grew up here, played varsity sports here, and had plotted his escape by way of an academic scholarship to the University of Virginia. It almost worked, but a suspicious incident in his senior year sent him back home in shame, and without a degree. Then, quite interestingly enough, a recruiter from the Central Intelligence Agency picked him up one day as he was thumbing for a ride along highway 267. The CIA's indoctrination and training center, known as "The Farm," was only a couple of hours away in Camp Peary, VA, so it seemed a plausible coincidence at the time.

Now, driving along the very same roadway, he knew the truth was something less coincidental. He knew it, because over forty years in the CIA as a field officer had given him a glimpse of reality. There were no coincidences when it came to the CIA. He had been manipulated, and very skillfully recruited.

Over the years, he had used very similar tactics to recruit assets of his own, in places like Cambodia and Laos, Nicaragua and Venezuela, Lebanon and Afghanistan. By the time he reached his sixties, Diggs had made the grand tour with the company.

He had also grown tired of the mission statement, and somewhere along the line realized that trying to save millions of people from harm was futile. It seemed a more focused approach, to simply eliminate the few who would do them harm. Which, after he left the agency, is what brought him to the attention of a beautiful young woman. A woman of extraordinary power and means. A woman who intended to change the world.

4

VENEZUELA

Camila was too young for her life to end this way. At only fourteen, she was just beginning to feel like a real person. Someone independent of her parents, of her family's history, and her father's status. She was just beginning to dream about making her own future in the world. A future as big as a little girl's imagination can conceive, which is very big.

By most standards of comparison, her life was already big. She lived in a lush private villa surrounded by flowering hibiscus, palm trees, and armed guards, just outside the congestion and dangers of Caracas, the capital city of Venezuela. She had a nanny who watched over her and attended to most of her needs when she was home for the weekends, and she attended a very exclusive private girls boarding school in Cumana, near the Caribbean coast and the luxury estates of Isla Margarita.

She was privileged, and more than that, privileged in a country where almost everyone else was starving to death.

The veil that kept her shielded from how other children lived, and died, was about to be torn away, and the truly violent and ugly nature of the world revealed to her.

Camila's father was Esteban Aguera, a wealthy businessman, and former officer in the military when Venezuela was still under the control of El Presidente Hugo Chavez. Now under the post-Chavez administration, he had kept a lower profile, preferring to be in private industry rather than government work. He was once a very close advisor to Chavez, but he held less favor with the new administration.

THE MOST CELEBRATED time in a Latin American girl's life is her fifteenth birthday. The revered Quinceañera celebration. It marks their personal transformation across the age boundary into womanhood. Parents are expected to throw a party that far exceeds any other event in her life. Even weddings pale in comparison to some Quinceañera bashes, and one of the oddest desires of many young girls in South America for their Quinceañera party is to replace it with a week-long trip to the magical kingdom, Disney World. Camila was no different.

Her father, Esteban, in his infinite generosity, had agreed to send Camila and six of her very best friends, along with a chaperone, not just to Disney, but to Disney Paris in Marne-la-Vallée, France. Her Quinceañera would have been remembered as the best ever. Only that none of them ever made it safely to France.

There was only one Mercedes SL 500 at his disposal, and six girls and a chaperone to transport to the Simon Bolivar Airport in Caracas, to catch the Air France night flight non-stop to Charles de Gaulle Airport in Paris. So, Esteban decided to hire an extended van and driver from the state-owned San Carlos Transport Company.

The driver arrived at the Santa Maria School for Girls precisely at 5:00 p.m. Turning in from the main road, he drove slowly up the winding entry through lush manicured gardens, and pulled around the circular drive, stopping in front of the old colonial mansion that served as the main building for the school. The head mistress of the school, the trip chaperone, and Camila and her friends were all waiting outside.

He stepped out and walked around to the sliding side door and opened it for the young ladies, then proceeded to attend to loading the pile of luggage that was stacked on the gravel driveway. As the seven chattering girls leaped in and squabbled over seats, he lifted twelve large, heavy suitcases into the open back storage compartment of the blue Ford Transit van.

He was shorter than most Venezuelans, but slender and fit. Very short-trimmed, black hair and a dark Caribbean tan that contrasted nicely with his pressed white shirt and brown slacks. He was handsome for a van driver, and the chaperone in charge of the girls, Silvia, an attractive, single woman in her early-thirties, noticed his muscular arms extending from the short sleeves, and also that he seemed particularly fascinated with his watch.

It was a very nice Tissot Divers watch, which seemed a bit out of place on the arm of van driver. She caught his eye, and he smiled and faintly canted his head to one side, then, distracted, Silvia stumbled as she caught her foot on the side step.

When the girls were all safely in their seats, the driver pulled the sliding door closed from the outside and climbed up into his seat, pulled his seatbelt around himself and clicked it snugly, then started up the Ford. It was going to be at least a two-hour drive to Caracas. Silvia was sitting in the first row behind the handsome driver. She leaned forward and lay her hand lightly on his elbow, "My name is Silvia, may I ask yours?"

He glanced up into the rearview mirror, and she

looked up and could see his dark eyes crinkle in the corners as he smiled again, "My name is Ramon. Encantado, Señorita," he said. By addressing her as "Señorita", he had obviously noticed that she wasn't wearing a wedding band.

She smiled as she sat back in her seat, excited at the prospect of meeting a handsome man within her same station in life. Reflexively, she reached up and touched her neck with the tips of her fingers, then unclasped the top pearl button of her blouse, as it suddenly felt like it was gripping her throat.

The young girls laughed and chatted and teased about what French boys might be like. They became more quiet after fifteen minutes of driving along the highway, catching glimpses to the right of the celeste blue sea, between the dense forest and occasional outcroppings of rural shacks and farm houses.

Forty-five minutes into the journey, they came to the small city of Barcelona, a quaint little town spread out along the coast, and vaguely reminiscent of the grand city in Spain that it was named after.

"We won't be able to stop again for over an hour, so we should stop here to use the restroom. Is that ok with everyone?" the driver said.

Most of the girls were already asleep, as they were so excited the night before, they didn't sleep at all. He heard Silvia answer, "Yes, please."

He turned and smiled at her again, and saw her

cheeks blush as he held her eye for just an instant. Then he looked at his watch once again, to make sure he was precisely on schedule.

"I know a nice hotel near the port where we can go, and the restrooms are very clean," he said. Then he pulled off the main road onto a dirt camino that went north, in the general direction of the sea.

Leaving the paved highway and scattered buildings of Barcelona, they were almost instantly driving through a jungle canopy that filtered the last remaining rays of a flaming red sunset. He twisted a knob on the dash and turned on the headlights, and the beams appeared to light the way through a cavern of green trees and tangled vines. A few times, small creatures scampered across the road, through the bluish halogen light.

After traveling three miles or so, Silvia asked, "Are you sure we are on the right road? It looks very deserted out here."

"Yes, very sure. We are almost there."

As they rounded a tight corner, a flash of lights suddenly lit the world around them and blinded Silvia. The one girl in front who was still awake at this point, shrieked, and Silvia gasped and brought her hand to her chest. The driver stood hard on the brakes, and the tires of the van slid and then chattered to a stop in the soft sand.

A cloud of dust from the road enveloped the van and clouded over the windows, and even the headlights became choked by the swirling fine sand. Silvia and the girls looked from side to side but couldn't see any further than the dark film that clung to the large glass windows.

The driver clicked his seatbelt loose, then cracked his door open so the overhead lights came on in the van. Camila and the rest of her friends were all awake now, and they watched in horror as he turned and smiled again at Silvia, then swiftly raised a compact .380 caliber automatic pistol and shot her point-blank in the face.

Silvia's head snapped backward, then slowly rolled to the left and down, until her chin was nestled in the open collar of her blouse. Her body seemed to shrink in size as the muscles relaxed, and only the shoulder restraint kept her from falling over.

The small hollow point bullet had been placed very precisely, expanded perfectly, and did not exit. Only the tiniest few drops of blood dribbled from the entry wound, down the front of Silvia's skirt before her heart stopped, and her circulatory system lacked the pressure to continue pumping.

Camila and her six best friends sat in stunned silence. They heard the thunder of feet approaching the van. The side door was suddenly ripped open on squealing rollers, and a smothering blanket of dust was sucked in the van and into their eyes and lungs.

Their screams echoed into the surrounding jungle.

The Ford Transit van was found three days after the seven girls disappeared. Several of the girls' families had been waiting at Simon Bolivar Airport to kiss their children one last time and wave as they left on their big adventure to Paris, but they never arrived.

The van was found resting fifteen feet below the surface of the sea, in a narrow bay that lay below a shallow cliff. The front end was wedged into a coral reef crevice, and the tail end pointing straight up to the surface. When the tide was fully out, the shining chrome bumper was barely visible above the waterline, and it caught the eye of a passing fisherman who was throwing a casting net for small baitfish. It was still in first gear, with a block of wood holding the accelerator pedal forward, when they hauled it up from the sea with a mobile crane.

The van held no clues about what might have happened to the girls. There were two things found in the van. First, the body of San Carlos Transport Company driver, Ramon Velasquez, in the driver seat. It was determined that he had been bludgeoned to death, with several crushing wounds about the head.

Second, was the body of Silvia, still strapped tightly into her seat, a long dark blue skirt and pink blouse soaked and clinging to her body. Her skin, once soft and tanned, was now the color of sterling silver that has been left neglected for years, gray and tarnished, and mottled with black and blue spots. Her head was hanging limply against her chest, and her wet hair was still wound and pinned in an elegant knot, which revealed the single, small caliber bullet wound just above her left eye.

5

CARACAS, VENEZUELA

For years, everyone had known the people abducting young girls were working for the drug cartels. The girls were usually moved from one place to another, as they drugged them, tortured them, and prepared to send them into servitude in one of thousands of brothels scattered about South America.

It was supplemental income for the cartels. Profits paled in comparison to the sale of narcotics, but it was very stable income, and very low risk.

Local police, prosecutors, judges, and public officials could all be easily bought off with a small amount of cash and services. The corruption permeated almost every level of society. And since most of the abductions were from lower-class barrios, it rarely made the news. Quite often, the police were never even called, because they would just dismiss it as a "runaway."

But in recent years, the legal prostitution market had been growing across many islands in the Caribbean, and young girls who met certain standards became more valuable. When the human trafficking market in the Caribbean became cross-pollinized with the well-established traffickers from the Middle East, the higher-ups in the world of corruption came to see it as a more profitable venue.

And now it seemed, with the abductions of seven girls from well-established families, they no longer cared about just preying on the weak and the poor. Three weeks had passed, and not a single ransom demand received, so, what else could it be?

MARIELLA MARTINEZ WASN'T GOING to let it go. The stonewalling, the delays, the denials. All of the normal ploys of the corrupt police and government officials, as they kept the truth from the people. The seven girls who vanished three weeks ago were from a social class that was higher than those normally afflicted, but for some reason their abductions had fortified the others.

The other families who searched in vain, and whose requests for records and search warrants were regularly blocked or delayed by judges on the payroll. Whose payroll, no one really knew for sure. All anyone knew, was that over three-thousand young girls vanished nearly every year from the cities and towns in Venezuela.

Mariella had been building and leading a coalition of families for the past two years, all of whom had lost children to this plague of corruption. They protested, they made claims to the media if they could get attention, and were beginning to become a nuisance to the officials of Caracas.

Mariella was tougher than she looked. She was petite, standing barely five-feet two inches if she leaned up on her toes. In her younger years she always kept her shining black hair long, but in these dark Maduro years, she had cut it into an efficient bob that just touched her narrow shoulders.

In healthier times, she weighed a little over one hundred pounds, but these were lean years, and at forty-seven-years old she probably had less than ninety on her now. But what she lacked in size or physical strength, she made up for with grit.

She was just thirty years old in 2002, when Hugo Chavez was nearly dethroned in an attempted coup d'etat, and she was working as a special assistant to one of the senior managers of the state-run oil company, PDVSA. After the failed coup, Chavez rounded up many of the oil company executives, whom he considered personal enemies, and imprisoned them, or simply made them disappear.

Mariella had been taken into custody along with her boss, and she survived seven months in the infamous *El Helicoide*, a private prison operated by the Intelligence and Security Services of Venezuela.

She was lucky to have lived and been set free, given that she was more deeply connected to the failed coup than anyone ever knew. In fact, there was only one man who knew who she really was. But that was then.

Now, Mariella was a fierce and very public activist. Challenging the corruption that covered for the cartels and those who steal young girls from the streets. And she had her reasons. She had once lost a child of her own. Not to the streets or the cartels, but to the dark chambers of *El Helicoide*. A child never born.

Last night she sat looking out the window of her tiny apartment, on the third floor of a dilapidated building in the hillside barrio known as El Valle. It was dark, save for a small candle burning on top of an upturned fruit crate that she used for a table. The breezeless heat was suffocating and empowered the stench of mold and rotting wood. She looked out over the lights of Caracas, stretching to the far horizon. There were patches of blackness where parts of the city, and millions of people, had no power.

Here and there, she could see flashes of light, like fireflies sprinkling the darkened barrios with sparkling fairy dust, and moments later, if she listened carefully, she could hear the faint taps of gunfire.

From this elevation she could almost see the top of

El Helicoide. It made her think of the child she lost. It made her think of *him*.

Then, in a moment of regret and sadness, she pulled out her worn Motorola cell phone and called a number that he encouraged her to memorize so many years ago. A number that she was only to call in a desperate situation, and one that she had never dialed before.

After seventeen years, she had no idea if the number still worked, but it rang three times, then a mechanical voice requested her to leave a message.

"Bill. This is Mariella. I should have told you something many years ago, but I was afraid." She hesitated for a minute. "I lost our child in *El Helicoide*. Please forgive me."

Then without leaving her number, she hung up. She knew the father of her lost child would never hear her words, but it didn't matter. She just needed to say them out loud, even if it was just to the answering machine of a wrong number. It made her feel slightly less burdened by guilt, at a time when she was unsure of how much longer she might be alive.

6

PORT D'ANDRATX, MALLORCA, SPAIN

When the first rays of sunlight broke over the eastern horizon and struck the tall Aleppo pines, they instantly cast a row of shadows over the terrace, like Spartans linked shoulder-to-shoulder preparing for the rush of battle. Lucas had seen many days of battle and shed the blood of many evil men.

He had killed warlords in the Central African Republic, Taliban in Afghanistan and terrorists in Iraq and Syria, and Taureg warriors and mercenaries in the coastal dunes of Algeria. And recently, a number of hired assassins and one very wealthy money launderer in Monaco.

Since 3:00 in the morning, some of the scenes had been replaying like a film reel in his head, over and over. Patiently waiting and watching, silently stalking his prey. Subconsciously synchronizing his movements, his breathing, his heartbeats, with those of the men he was about to kill.

Some were targets of pure chance and opportunity. He killed them with rudimentary implements like hammers and fishing knives stolen from a truck parked by the marina. Others were more calculated, planned. Professionally executed attacks, interrogations, and murders.

Twelve years ago, at a time when he felt like his life had ended before it had begun, when he was really just a boy, he signed his life over to the Legion. "Make me brave and strong," he begged. "Or let me die a hero's death."

Try as he might, he had failed to be a hero and save his little sister, Eliza, from being abducted when she was only eleven, and he was just seventeen. He lay beaten in the dirt and watched, as the Moroccan henchmen sped away with her.

But fate has a way of seeking out the bold.

Fate kept him alive through twelve years of war across the African continent, as the French Foreign Legion honed him into a surgically-sharp instrument of death. Fate brought him back to the world, and back to his home in Mallorca, and the real purpose of his life unfolded before his eyes.

The winds of fortune gave him a second chance, and by the time he was done, everyone who had a hand in his sister's disappearance was dead. They were all dead, and his sister, miraculously, was still alive. More than alive, she had turned her own bad fortune to her favor, and now wielded power and influence. Like Lucas, she had risen from the ashes.

She also had scores of her own to settle, and a chance encounter with legendary CIA officer, Bill Diggs, led to a unique union, her access to wealth and nefarious men, and his intimate knowledge of making them disappear.

The Fairhope Group was born. Its purpose was a simple one: identify and target the truly despicable people who live above the law and prey on the rest of the world. Not to bring them to justice, but to put them in the ground.

The first person they searched for to bring into the Group, was Lucas, who by now was a hardened killer in the service of the Legion. And now, having proven that he was up to the task, it was time for Lucas to take the reins.

THE SEA WAS QUIET TODAY. The surface flat and silent, like a deep green lap pool, stretching to the far horizon. Barely a perceptible ripple here and there from the small fish coming to the surface in the early morning hours, to sip morsels from the settling film. But the Mediterranean never stayed still for long. For thousands of years, she'd lured men to the deep, then crushed them without warning. Lucas smiled. It reminded him of his little sister.

He was sitting in his favorite teak chair on the very edge of the stone terrace, looking out over the sugar-sand beach of Port d'Andratx below. The villa that was once the summer home of his family in happier times, was now his shelter from the rest of the world. It was the one place he could take a deep breath and let his mind wander. Lately, it wandered to the only other woman who ever occupied his thoughts, Avigail.

He didn't know her long enough to even know her last name, although she never used it. She, too, had been taken from her home as a child, and sold into the human-trafficking markets in Algiers, many years before. Unbeknownst to Lucas, she was still trapped in that world of bondage and obligation to a brutal master, when he met her in Monte Carlo, three months before.

She seduced him, then set him up to be killed. And yet, his heart felt more than just compromised. It felt captured. He couldn't stop thinking about her.

7

CARACAS, VENEZUELA

Mariella was concerned about the protest they had planned. She had contacted a reporter at the largest newspaper, El Diario Caracas, and told them she had evidence that Judge Marco Jimenez had predictably withheld search warrants of known cartel brothels for three days, every time one was brought before his court.

She had organized a protest at the steps of the courthouse, Palacio de Justicia, on Avenida Bolivar. They were going to demand answers from the judge himself ,as he left the building in the afternoon, and it would make a great story for the paper. The reporter assured her he would be there and bring a camera crew to film them as they confronted the judge.

But the protests of all kinds in Venezuela were beginning to enrage El Presidente Maduro. Everywhere he looked, people were protesting the lack of food, or water, or electricity. And Maduro had spies. Loyal little spies in every corner of the block, videotaping and turning in organizers and rabble-rousers. They were paid well for turning people in to the FAES, more commonly known as the National Police Death Squad.

Only one week ago, a neighbor of Mariella was snatched from his hovel in the middle of the night, by men dressed in black armor, and he never came home. Mariella was worried that her unrelenting activism had made her a target.

The next afternoon, Mariella looked out over the street very carefully from her window before climbing down the rusty metal ladder to the side alley. The main stairwell in the building had been blocked off years before. It was quiet for a Monday, but it was past noon, and the midday heat kept people in the shadows.

She walked along the garbage-filled sidewalk, stepping over bags and bottles, and puddles of human waste, until she reached the outer edge of the barrio, where the *perreras* (dog cages) would pass by every hour.

Most of the city bus lines had broken down years ago and were never repaired, so industrious people who owned pickup trucks put large wire cages around the beds (which really look like dog cages), and now made a living by cramming standing passengers into the back and delivering them around town. There would often be up to twenty people smashed like sardines into the truck cages, and several more hanging off the sides as they wheeled around the city.

The one Mariella climbed onto went directly to the Palacio de Justicia. It was nearly to capacity already, but she handed the driver a few coins and walked to the back. An older man, with gray whiskers and soiled clothes, pushed back against the boys behind him to make just enough room for one more pair of small feet, and a young man perched on the rear bumper reached out his hand and helped her into the truck bed.

Many of the passengers with her were going to the courthouse to see relatives who had been charged with crimes. They were among the poorest and forgotten of a country that held riches in oil just below the surface. None had bathed in months, except when the heavy rains came, and they shed their clothes to stand in the falling deluge. But they were used to the odor of close company, and the fumes of automobiles and belching diesel trucks was more overpowering than that of human sweat.

The *perrera* swayed and teetered under the load of bodies as it navigated down the hillside into the city center, grinding the frame and sparking against the pavement over undulating sections. It made two more stops, where people got off and new ones got on, then it precariously tilted up on two wheels as it turned the corner onto Avenida Bolivar. The riders were all so accustomed, that no one seemed alarmed.

Three blocks more, and the driver began to slow down to a crawl as they approached the courthouse. The rusty brakes squealed as he pressed down hard to stop the overloaded truck, and the hangers-on started leaping off before it came to a full stop.

No one heard the motorcycle engine revving up as it darted from traffic behind the *perrera* and came speeding to catch up, with a driver and passenger, both dressed in all black with full-faced helmets. As they came alongside, the passenger pulled his backpack off his right shoulder, and slung it beneath the crusty old truck that was still packed with men, women, and at least two small children. Then the motorcycle accelerated furiously and sped away.

LUCINDA MORALES, a seventy-eight year old grandmother, was standing on the top step of the Judicial building, waiting for her son to be released from a petty theft charge. She was two-hundred and ten feet from the epicenter of the blast. She never heard the explosion, as the concussion wave struck first, after she saw the blinding white light.

Had she lived, she would have described the sensation as being hit by a speeding locomotive. The force of the blast wave crushed all of her internal organs, lifted her into the air, and sent the frail old woman crashing through the one-inch-thick safety glass in the front of the Judicial building. She was the closest casualty to the explosion, whose remains were found fully intact. Anyone closer than that, was found in pieces, or not at all.

The *perrera*, a 1979 Ford F100 pickup, disintegrated. Remnant parts were discovered up to a half mile from the scene. No one will ever know for sure how many people were actually on the back, because there were not enough remains of any to identify them all, except from personal items, or wallets or purses that contained identification cards that hadn't been completely vaporized or engulfed in flame. Tattered shreds of clothing and strips of flesh were hanging from the trees and plastered against the sides of the buildings along the block.

8

GIBRALTAR

Constantino Gallo stood on the third floor balcony, looking out over the threshold of the Mediterranean Sea and Atlantic Ocean. Rolling waves of azure blue that faded to purple and gray. Others marveled at this view, but Constantino hated the fucking sea. And yet it seemed, he had spent most of his life living next to it; the coast of Spain, France, and now Gibraltar. He couldn't seem to escape the sight of water and waves, and the ever-present pungent stink of salty fish.

Behind him, the thirteen-hundred and eighty-five foot high limestone rock blotted out the sky. The famous Rock of Gibraltar, a world-renowned, and frequently fought-over landmark, but to him it was just a rock that smelled like monkey shit from the free-roaming macaques that the tourists adored.

He wasn't a man who saw wonder in many things.

Only the sight and smell of money captured his attention.

His home was a meticulously restored British colonial mansion that sat just down the block from the entrance to the Governor's mansion, on a wide flower-lined avenue, one of the few peaceful driving and walking lanes in the congested capital port town. Prime real estate in a beautiful setting, but again, Constantino resented being relegated to this island. It was a prison whose only saving grace was the shield provided by its British landlords. The shield of privacy for illicit businesses, and no taxes of any kind.

Constantino's business was laundering and hiding the wealth of the richest most vile men in the world, and business was good.

He was tall and Spanish handsome, with an angular jaw line, olive skin, and black hair that was recently beginning to fade to silver in the temples. He was not quite sixty, but had aged rapidly in the previous decade, and looked a few years beyond it. Uncharacteristically for a handsome man, he no longer cared to flaunt his looks and charm. He was no longer the peacock, but rather, a vulture.

The world had been cruel to Constantino, and it changed him. Once a man of family and friendships, now he sought only power, and his thoughts were consumed by a simmering resentment that boiled below his calm facade. Resentment for what, exactly, he couldn't say. Maybe for everything. Everything he lost, everything he wanted, everything around him.

FROM THE BALCONY he heard the telephone ring twice in his office before his assistant answered. Then her tall heels came tapping toward the open French doors, "Señor Gallo, a gentleman calls from Beirut. Would you like to accept the call, or should I take a message?"

He turned quickly away from the view and came through the doors, "I'll take the call, Porsche."

"Very well, sir. He waits on line one. Will you be needing anything else?"

"No, close the office door as you leave."

He waited until he was alone before picking up the elegant silver-handled receiver, "Good afternoon." He didn't bother asking who the caller was, because only one person in Beirut had the number to his direct line.

A man with a crisp, baritone voice, speaking in a French-Arabic dialect, said, "Constantino, our Persian partners will soon have need of a new transitional account."

"How will the account be used?" Constantino asked.

"For deposits and dispersion of assets to other companies," the voice answered.

"Do you have preferences for the destination of this account, and the currency?"

"Yes. Curaçao, and in dollars."

"Curaçao is no problem. I can have an account ready for transactions in two days."

The voice responded, "This is a unique situation, Constantino. We are sending an emissary for the final trade negotiations, and due to the size and nature of the initial deposits, we will require you to be there to personally verify the account access, the deposit, and assist with setting up a line of credit to draw against it."

Constantino was silent, and unsure how to respond. He had never been required to physically verify an account, and after all, virtually all of the accounts that he managed for his clients were in scattered "haven" locations. The physical location of the banks' offices meant very little in this day and age, because once the initial deposits were made, the wealth became digital and highly mobile.

That was the point - to convert the wealth into a form that was easy to funnel through the laundromat of corporate investment vehicles and have instant access from anywhere in the world with nothing but a username and passcode.

Constantino frequently traveled to meet his clients in their home countries - the UAE, Algeria, Morocco, Dubai, Lebanon, even a few visits to South Africa, the Sudan and recently, Belgium. But physically walking into a tax-sheltering bank and verifying deposits would put him at great risk of losing his anonymity, and anonymity kept him alive.

"That isn't a service I normally provide," he answered.

"This is not a request for services, Constantino. You serve at our will. You draw breath every single day, only because we allow it. Don't ever forget that." The Arab-speaker paused, then added, "Remember, 'Constantino' was not always your name, and you were not always as rich as you are now. We made you who you are, and we can unmake you just as quickly."

And there it was, the threat that he always knew was there, but was never before spoken. He had become complacent with his role. Managing and manipulating the profits of vice and crime, and war and terror, on a grand scale. He was an extraordinarily wealthy man, but in the scheme of things, he was just the bean counter for the lords of true fortune, the merchants of very profitable evil.

He acquiesced, "I understand, sir. When should I arrive in Curaçao?"

"We are sending our emissary from Marrakesh in ten days. I believe you know him from your work with Farouk. His name is Aziz Harrak."

"I have never met him, but I know who he is. He assumed responsibility for the Morocco supply chain, before Farouk was assassinated, and I manage all of the financial assets in his distribution network."

Like most of the pieces of Hezbollah's network, their operations were kept highly compartmentalized, and men within the network frequently didn't know each other. Suspicion of everyone not personally known, was an effective means of vetting potential spies.

"I will send details of the meeting in Curaçao to you within the next twenty-four hours. You may arrange your own travel, but keep me advised."

9

TEL AVIV, ISRAEL

"Commander Moskarov, we just received an urgent communication from the surveillance team in Gibraltar," the young Lieutenant said as he entered the office. He handed the folded envelope across the desk and stood crisply at attention.

"Stand at ease, Lieutenant," his commanding officer said as he opened the letter and read it silently. When he finished, he turned and fed the paper into a shredder. "It's on. The final negotiation is happening in ten days in Curaçao."

"We'll be taking action, won't we sir? We can't allow the Lebanese or the Iranians to profit from an alliance like that."

"We won't allow it, Lieutenant. But we won't take action unless it becomes necessary. Actually, I have a better idea."

Eli Moskarov would have never been mistaken for an Israeli. He was tall and muscular, had a fair complexion, and wispy blonde hair that was quickly receding at the temples. He had a large angular jaw and firm brow, and celeste blue eyes that, on a woman, might have been considered extraordinarily beautiful. But when Eli stared in your direction, they were penetrating, like icy spikes running through the deepest part of your soul.

He never smiled, never looked happy. He looked Russian. And in fact, he was born and raised in St. Petersburg, in a poverty-stricken neighborhood bordering the village of Pushkin, which probably explained why he was rarely happy.

The only thing that made Eli happy, was killing enemies of Israeli. Despite his Russian origins, Eli was born a Jew, and his mother had raised him to feel a deep connection with his people. After watching his parents suffer and die at the hands of the old KGB before the USSR collapsed, he escaped alone at the age of fourteen and emigrated to Israel.

At eighteen, he entered the military for his two years of mandatory service, and was then recruited directly into the Israeli Mossad. He spent almost twenty-five years in the field, working mostly in northern Europe, Scandinavia, and the United States.

His distinctive appearance made it difficult for him to blend into the scenery in places like North Africa and the Mediterranean.

Over the years, Eli had forged a number of working relationships with men and women in other agencies; MI6, French Intelligence, and the CIA in particular. It was his relationship with one officer in the CIA that had drawn his attention last year and instigated a new surveillance operation. An operation that led to a spiderweb of illicit businesses, all being operated for the financial benefit of one of Israel's greatest threats - Hezbollah.

Bill Diggs was unaware that his old friend, Eli had been watching his movements back and forth around the Middle East and the Med. He was unaware that Eli was preparing to take direct action on a wealthy financier in Monaco, after uncovering billions of dollars in transactions for North African clients who all had ties to Beirut and Iran. Until, that is, someone else took action ahead of him.

It was then he uncovered the ex-CIA operative's connection to a mysterious new organization known as, the Fairhope Group. At first, he was confused by the murders of Moroccan thugs, organized crime bosses, a Monte Carlo banker, and the Algerian Ambassador to Spain. Was it a power play? A coup d'etat in the making?

But none of it fit. Then, it came to him. His old

friend, Bill Diggs wasn't in the game anymore. He didn't have a long term political agenda. He was just systematically eliminating men who all had connections to horrific crimes against humanity. He'd gone rogue.

"LIEUTENANT, do you still have eyes on Bill Diggs?"

"Yes sir, the morning report had him arriving at Dulles Airport in Washington D.C., but he didn't go to Langley."

"No. He's not officially part of the agency anymore. He probably went home to Winchester. Find him and arrange for one of our local Virginia assets to hand-deliver a correspondence."

"Yes, sir."

ELI, opened the top drawer of his desk and pulled out a file. It was thin with information, and so new it still had the waxy sheen on the exterior surface. It was the file of someone he hoped to use one day as an asset for Israel.

After the assassination of the Algerian Ambassador three months ago, a very wonderful gift landed at Eli's feet. A beautiful young woman, plucked from the sea immediately after the Ambassador's yacht exploded and sank beneath the waves. A woman who had spent almost her entire life as a slave to a man imbedded in the world of Islam, and an integral part of his life and business operations. And as it turned out, a woman who was also born a Jew, right here in Tel Aviv.

Her name was Avigail.

10

WINCHESTER, VIRGINIA

Bill Diggs was almost home. The car turned off Highway 267 and followed a two-lane country road, twisting through a mix of farms and horse pastures, crumbling farm houses and barns, and signs of more modern homes sprinkled across the hill crest.

Diggs was surprised when the driver pulled into the overgrown gravel drive and up to the old house without his direction. Even this old place, the place he thought as a boy was in the middle of nowhere and outside the view or care of God, even this was now easily found on Google Maps. He had nowhere left to hide.

The old house was a typical clapboard square. The tin roof was twenty years past expiration and the rust stains bled down the sides and over the rotting side boards. What little paint was left had yellowed, and the honeysuckle vines grew wild along the south face. The front porch was leaning prominently to the right, and the boards were rain-soaked and covered in green moss. Bill was the third generation Diggs to own the old house, and likely the last.

He tipped his driver, slung his bag over his shoulder and stepped carefully up the mushy planks on the porch, then tested the front door handle. It was unlocked and turned easily enough, but the door was swollen from the rains, so he gave it a shove with his shoulder and it swung open on squeaky hinges. It smelled damp and musty inside, like an opium cave in the Cambodian jungle he remembered from 1975.

As infinitely detailed as Diggs' memory was, he couldn't remember the last time he was here. Nothing had changed. It looked precisely as it always had.

Pictures of family, dead for decades, sat on the sideboard table. An old lamp that was ugly in 1949, still perched on the round table by the window, and the sofa that his mother loved, the only fine thing she had ever owned in her lifetime, rested in the exact position as the day it came to the house.

It was like crossing through a veil to another time. A time when life was more simple, and his family still lived. But everything that represented his heritage was yellowing as the years passed, or being swallowed by the dust and webs of nature.

. . .

Diggs went for a run at 10:00 pm, following the dirt road down to the river, crossing the old wooden bridge and the green patina'd monument that stood proudly in the field, designating it as a Civil War battlefield. Then he looped back over the elm tree ridge in the dark on an old hunting trail. He used it so many times as a kid, that he could do it even without the moonlight assistance he had tonight.

Evening runs were a routine for him. Everything he did was done in precisely ordered routines. He rose at exactly 4:50 every morning. He ate at the same time, and usually the same thing unless he was out on mission. He checked his gear, his weapons, reset his watch, and before driving anywhere he did a full "pre-flight" level inspection on his vehicle. Engine oil, battery, tire pressure, suspension, warning lights, and let it idle for ten minutes to check the running temperature.

Details make a difference when your life might depend on them, and he had managed to live a very long time in a very dangerous occupation. He managed his fitness the same way, and at sixty-five he was slender and hard. Still viable for field duty.

He was pouring his first cup of black coffee at 0510 when his cell phone rang. He pushed the green button and brought it to his ear, but didn't speak. He never liked to be the first one to make a move.

"Bill Diggs?" a voice asked.

Again, Diggs stayed silent, waiting for more

information about the caller before offering any of his own. Only a few people had his number, and this didn't sound like any of them.

"Bill, it's Mathew Penn. Stop playing games."

He answered, "Matt from Caracas?"

"The very same, Amigo."

"Been a long time. I heard you were promoted to Station Chief. Congratulations. How did you get this number, Matt? Never mind, stupid question." he said. "It's a little early for a friendly reunion, isn't it?"

"I knew you'd be awake. And this isn't a reunion call, Bill."

"Tell me what it is then."

"Did you see the news a few days ago about the truck bomb in Caracas? The one in front of the Judicial complex?"

"I don't watch the news anymore, Matt. And besides there are ten bombings every day around Venezuela. They don't even cover them all on the news."

"Yeah, it's a real monkey-shit-fight down here right now. And this bomb was the biggest turd that's been thrown lately."

Diggs thought for a moment before asking the next question, "So what does this have to do with an old retired guy like me?"

"You were running the NCS desk down here in 2002 during the Chavez coup, right?" (The NCS, National Clandestine Service, was created by

President George W. Bush and granted total domain over human clandestine intelligence gathering. They ran the CIA's psychological and paramilitary ops under complete deniability.)

"Didn't you have a civilian asset inside the economic group? A woman named Mariella Martinez?"

Diggs straighten up and tensed his jaw. He hadn't heard or spoken her name in almost seventeen years. Out of the dozens of assets he had cleverly recruited and used in the performance of his duties, she was the only one who haunted him. He could feel his stomach twisting in knots, and braced himself for what he might hear next.

"What about her?"

"She was on the truck, Bill."

He swallowed hard, and took a deep breath, "It's a common name, there must be fifty-thousand Mariella Martinezes in that country. How can you be so sure it was the same woman?"

"We found a small purse with an I.D., and ran it through our database. We're sure. And not only that, but I think she was the primary target. She's the only one we can identify who was pissing off the local crime lords. Mariella had turned into a serious activist. She was organizing protests, media coverage, and doing everything she could to make life tough for some of the local politicians and judges."

"Matt, everyone in that fucking country is

protesting right now. What was she protesting that set them off?"

"Kidnappings. It's not exactly something new here, but she was getting pretty aggressive about challenging the system, and the lack of response to young girls being snatched off the street." He paused for a second, then told him the rest, "Bill, there's something else. Four days ago, an old asset-message line went active. It should have been shut down years ago, but I guess it just fell through the cracks. Anyway, there was a message left. A message from Mariella, to you."

Diggs sat down at the small round table in his kitchen and stared out the window into the morning darkness.

Some things, no matter how long ago they happened, maintain a sharp cutting edge. They stay fresh in the mind, like it was only yesterday, and the wounds they leave never seem to heal. He could see his own reflection staring back in the dirty window, with a critical gaze. His residual self-image was gone. That image of himself as a young, strong man. He looked old, suddenly very old and tired.

He'd fallen into the trap only one time in forty years with the CIA. The snare that ruins careers like his. Falling in love with an asset. He had loved Mariella. Deeply and passionately. And yet, he still sent her into the lion's den, and she paid the price.

After the failed coup in 2002, to remove Hugo

Chavez from power, Diggs' job was done in Caracas, but he stayed for six months, waiting, watching, and leveraging contacts inside the hell-hole that was *El Helicoide*. He'd taken cash reserves and bribed the right people, and made sure Mariella was released. But he never had the courage to face her again.

He watched her from afar for three more weeks. She stayed with her mother, coming outside into the sunlight only a few times, then disappearing again. He left Caracas in late 2002, in the middle of the night, on a company plane to Cypress.

"Bill, are you still there?"

"I'm here."

"This might be a lot bigger than just the current Presidente trying to shut up a few activists. We're still looking into it."

Diggs hesitated, he wasn't sure how much the CIA knew about him, the Fairhope Group, and their recent hunting activities in the Mediterranean.

"Listen Bill, I'll get my ass in a real crack if anyone finds out I let you listen to this. I'm going to play the message one time, then I'm going to scrub the recorder and shut the line down." He played the message.

His reaction was one Diggs had never had before. It was like a hot poker of acid rushing up from his belly, and the burn of bile hitting the back of his throat. Beads of sweat instantly appeared on his forehead, and he felt like he was going to pass out.

Then it changed. He felt the switch flip in his head, and the sick, weak, emotional moment passed. Now he was calm. Calm, and ready to kill someone.

"I'll be on the ground in Caracas in twenty-four hours."

Mathew Penn responded, "Send me an encrypted message with your arrival plans, and I'll have someone meet you."

II

CARACAS, VENEZUELA

Esteban Aguera tried to swallow, but he hadn't a drop of saliva. The inside of his mouth felt like sunbaked leather, and his throat was coated with a scratching grit that made speaking almost impossible. It didn't matter that much; his only real job at the moment was to listen, not speak.

For the first time in his entire life, he was sitting in the presence of a man he truly feared. A man who could, and would if it pleased him, snuff out his life if he didn't get precisely what he wanted. And afterwards, just for the pleasure, he would personally see to the demise of Esteban's entire known family, beginning with his daughter, Camila. The man's name was Raphael Ortega.

Raphael looked carefully at his watch, then made a note of the time in a small notebook sitting on the table in front of him, "The Intelligence Directorate was very appreciative of your support in identifying the spy. Mariella Martinez' treachery cost the lives of sixteen of our patriots who were all here to support your 'El Commandante,' when the capitalists were trying to murder him."

Esteban smiled vaguely, and acknowledged with a slight nod of his head, but didn't speak.

"We are curious though, why it took so many years for you to bring this to our attention?"

Esteban tried to clear his throat and started to speak, but the Cuban operative halted him with a wave of his hand and continued, "We'll come back to that at another time. For now, I need to be assured that you understand exactly what we require."

Esteban acknowledged with a definitive nod.

"Your existing network and delivery capabilities to the United States will be very beneficial to securing an agreement with our new business partners from the Middle East. And, naturally, you will share in the proceeds."

Raphael paused, looked at his watch once again, then made additional notes. He was precise, attentive to the smallest detail, and missed nothing in the responses, gestures, and body language of the man sitting in front of him.

RAPHAEL ORTEGA HAD HAD to fight almost every day of his youth. He had been, for a time at least, a boy without a country, and the other boys in his barrio never let him forget it. They chased him, harassed him, and beat him mercilessly, until the day came when he would be beaten no more.

Raphael's parents were Castro-era Cubans, who jumped at the chance to leave their island home and flee to the United States in April of 1980, on the Mariel Boatlift, along with 125,000 others. They settled in a run-down neighborhood outside Hialeah, Florida, which later became known as "Little Havana". Raphael was born in the Hialeah General Hospital in 1981, one of the first natural Americans born to boatlift refugees.

But life in Florida never quite lived up to the dreams of Raphael's parents. His father had lived mostly as a petty thief back in Havana, and his trade brought him quickly onto the criminal justice system's radar in Miami.

On December 14, 1984, the United States and Cuba reached an agreement. Up to twenty-thousand Cubans would be allowed to legally immigrate to the United States annually to reunite with extended families and begin more prosperous lives in the USA. But, two-thousand seventy-six refugees from the original boatlift would be repatriated to Cuba. Some willingly, who longed for home; others, not so willingly. Raphael's parents fell into the latter category. Their son, even though born as a natural US Citizen, went back to the island with his parents.

And so, a four-year-old Cuban-American boy found himself living in a squalid barrio on the edge of Havana, in a crumbling apartment with no air-conditioning or running water. He slept on a grass-filled mattress, sewn together from discarded burlap potato sacks, and spent the nights listening to the skitter of rodents around the room and over his bed. He wore the same clothes every day, and while his mother worked hard to keep them clean, new clothes had to be stolen when he grew out of the ones he had.

He was neither Cuban nor American any longer. And seemingly wanted by neither country.

When he turned twelve, he was finally rewarded with full citizenship to Cuba, and by then he had fought his way through the worst of the bullies within a ten mile radius. He was a battle-hardened warrior before he hit puberty. And like all warriors, the endless fighting had removed the weakness and impractical aspects of his nature. Things like empathy, sympathy, and mercy no longer existed in his young soul. He was cold and mechanical.

With citizenship, Cuba had finally opened its arms to young Raphael and taken him in, and in many ways, she became more like a parent and guardian to him than any he had before. He embraced his new heritage and learned to loath the capitalists who had cast him out when he was still a boy.

In his secondary school years, Raphael showed an interest in history and sociology, and his marks were good enough to gain entry into the University of Havana in 1998. Two years later, he was forcibly recruited and transferred to a very special academy where he began doing research on counterintelligence, from a sociological perspective. He remained there for five more years until his graduation, at which time, the training for his real profession began in earnest.

In 2005, Raphael officially entered into the service of the Cuban Intelligence Directorate (DI), and was given the rank of lieutenant. It was only then that he was sent to Camp Matanzas, to learn the tradecraft that would make him one of the most lethal counterintelligence agents in the world.

Camp Matanzas is a highly secured training camp, hidden deep in the jungles and mangrove swamps of north-central Cuba. This is the training camp that has produced some of the most feared assassins the world has ever known. It's the Cuban equivalent of the CIA's "The Farm" in Camp Peary, Virginia.

Cuba has very little in the way of traditional military might, and other than heavily regulated and embargoed tourism, has little other industry to generate revenue. So over the past five decades, the Cuban DI has become something of a profitable export. Sending agents who are highly skilled in counterintelligence, assassinations, enhanced interrogation, and social manipulation, has become a specialty. And they get paid quite handsomely for their services.

Raphael Ortega was a particularly skilled DI operative. Cutting his teeth early on in Argentina, he counseled small town socialist organizers in the methods of intimidation and influencing local elections. He taught them how to organize protests, interrupt the flow of commerce by barricading roadways with picket lines, cause social disorder, and instigate fear and mistrust of democratically elected officials who didn't support the Leftist agenda.

In 2011, at the request of Iran's Revolutionary Guard, he was sent to Lebanon to supervise and train a number of regional recruits in a Hezbollah training camp. He taught them the most brutal and effective methods of enhanced interrogations and highly specialized assassination techniques.

The DI had been very careful to maintain his cover as nothing more than an advisor, everywhere he worked, but the trail of bodies and high-profile disappearances that followed his travels was hard to miss.

Provincial politicians who mysteriously drowned while trout fishing in shallow mountain streams. Federal prosecutors on the eve of delivering the biggest cases in their careers, committing suicide with a firearm that had never been seen before. The list of coincidental deaths was extensive.

Raphael was the most talented killer to come out of Camp Matanzas since Carlos the Jackal.

And now, Raphael Ortega was staring directly into the eyes of a desperate man. The father of a young girl who vanished into thin air several weeks ago. A man who also, conveniently enough, had precisely the business background and infrastructure in place to cement a very lucrative agreement for the Cuban Intelligence Directorate.

The DI was in the final negotiation stage of a strategic alliance with another ambitious group on the other side of the Atlantic, Hezbollah. An alliance that would raise significant capital for both. Hezbollah needed cash to wage war against the Israelis, and Cuba needed money to wage war against the capitalists of the United States.

"THIS IS GOING to be a historic alliance," Raphael said. "Venezuela will prosper, Cuba will prosper, and you will prosper."

"The Chinese have been cultivating this channel for their opioids for several years, Raphael. They aren't going to be happy about the competition," Esteban said.

"Fuck the Chinese. They are moving more fake

fentanyl through the Mexican cartels than they can make now. They don't need this channel, and none of what they are selling is benefiting the Venezuelan people, or my people. Russian and Persian partners will be a better fit for your country."

Esteban was starting to relax. He realized that his expertise and his delivery infrastructure were essential to making this alliance work. "When will I be able to see my daughter."

"Camila is safe. And she will remain safe as long as you provide a reliable delivery channel for the drugs. But if anything happens that jeopardizes this alliance, Camila will be sold in a street market in Marrakesh. Do you understand?"

Esteban clenched his teeth and held his voice. Very few men had ever spoken to him this way and lived to talk about it, and he had a natural hatred for the Cuban DI operatives who prowled around the Venezuelan capital like they owned it. He would kill them all if he got the chance. But for now, all he could do was nod his head and swallow his pride.

"If everything is working well over the next year, then we'll talk more about Camila. Until then, stay focused on your job."

ESTEBAN WAS A STEREOTYPE. A ruggedly handsome, mustachioed Latino, early fifties, skin bronzed from the weekends spent aboard his sailing yacht harbored in Isla Margarita.

Back in the golden days of Hugo Chávez, Esteban had been a major asset to the Bolivarian Revolution. As a young man in the Venezuelan Army, he idolized Chavez, and became a devoted loyalist. He thrived in the new regime and was quickly promoted into the Venezuelan Military Intelligence Directorate.

As Venezuela's oil business began to dwindle, and pressure from the United States mounted, the VMID devised a plan to disrupt social order in the United States, and get rich in the process. They were going to deluge American cities with cocaine.

The military officers involved in the plan, including Esteban Aguera, came to be known as, "The Cartel of the Suns." A tongue in cheek reference to the sun insignia on the Venezuelan generals' uniforms.

Cocaine was sourced by trading weapons, ammunition, and guerrilla training from Cuban operatives, to the FARC rebels in neighboring Columbia. It effectively killed two birds with one stone, by destabilizing the rival nation's government and focusing attention from the United States somewhere else. The drugs were funneled through various delivery routes, air, land, and sea. Esteban's responsibility was the sea.

Over the years, he cultivated reliable methods for moving tons of cocaine across the Caribbean to dealer networks in Miami, Key West, Cocoa Beach, and Fort Meyers. Using multiple boats as decoys, he created a complex shell-game for the DEA and Coast Guard that was rarely bested.

When Chávez died, Esteban saw the handwriting on the wall. He had always hated the Cuban DI's involvement in Venezuelan affairs, and he saw them becoming more influential with every day that passed. So he started padding his own retirement account, skimming and accumulating assets, property, and building his own enterprise as the leader of a private drug cartel, but he would always be known as an original member of the Cartel of the Suns.

"MY TRANSPORTATION and supply chain into Florida is flawless. I can assure you there won't be any issues. The product will be selling through a chain of rural medical clinics and street dealers in fourteen states, within forty-eight hours of landing.

I also have resources for making very legitimate looking deposits into corporate accounts in New York, which will then funnel the money to offshore accounts. The days are long gone when we had to haul back sealed pallets of cash in submarines," Esteban said.

"What method will you use to move the merchandise to Florida?" Raphael asked.

"We have returned to the most cost effective and reliable method we ever used, very fast boats with professional drivers. Airplanes have become a prime target for the DEA, and there are no longer any safe landing zones. Submersibles were slow and never very effective at fooling radar. But a driver who can use the islands for cover and can drive at a high rate of speed, will vanish into the myriad of other boat traffic along the coast. Combined with some expensive intelligence about the ocean patrol activities of U.S law enforcement, it is over ninety-eight percent reliable."

"What about the other two percent of the time?"

"Two percent is an acceptable loss rate when the product brings twenty-fold returns."

Raphael made additional notes, then checked the time again. "One more thing, I will need for you to arrange a delivery of a smaller cargo to a private port east of Havana. This delivery must be one-hundred percent guaranteed."

"What's the cargo?"

"That's none of your concern. Can you do this, or do I need to find someone else?"

"I'll need to know how much it weighs, what the physical dimensions are, if it needs special protection from the salt air. If I don't have more information, I can't guarantee the delivery. However, the distance is not far, and there are no sea-based patrols until after a boat passes Cuba. The DEA might have air patrols or drones in use, but they would have no means of stopping us before entering Cuban territorial waters."

"The cargo isn't hazardous, but it will weigh a little over two tons, packed into sixteen small crates."

Esteban stared into his eyes for only three seconds before blurting out the answer, "You're moving a shipment of gold."

Raphael smiled, "You are very quick, Esteban. Yes, we are moving a small amount of gold bars from the island of Curaçao to the facilities at Camp Matanzas in Cuba. And can you guess what will happen to you if anything happens to that shipment?"

12

WINCHESTER, VIRGINIA

Diggs walked through the kitchen of the old farm house, and the warped floor boards groaned beneath his feet. He stopped and pushed down on one particular board and listened to the rusty nail squeaking underneath. The sound made him smile. Even though he hadn't had much to smile about in years and couldn't remember ever being happy in this house.

It brought back a memory; a vision of him as a boy trying to sneak up on his mother while she was cooking breakfast. That same loose board had given him away countless times, and yet his mother always feigned surprise.

He opened the door that led down to the cellar, reached up and pulled the chain to turn on the small incandescent bulb, then went down the staircase. Even though he hadn't lived here in years, he always kept a quick-travel bag in the cellar. He kept one in every location in the world he might visit or find himself in need of tools of the trade.

He pulled the carry-on size duffel out from under the roll-way bed and unzipped it. It looked like everything was still there. Clothes, boots, passports, two burner phones, rolls of cash in three types of currency, and a cosmetic kit with simple items to alter his appearance. There was also a Benchmade folding tactical knife, and a compact Glock 27 pistol in .40 caliber. He pulled the knife and pistol out and stashed them back under the bed. He needed to travel fast and keep his bag with him on the plane. Other weapons could be requisitioned at his destination.

He was still kneeling on the floor when he stopped dead still, listening. The old house made constant noise. Always shifting, settling, weak framing moving in the wind, but he heard something else. Something other than the house speaking its normal language.

He pulled the Glock back out, pressed the slide rearward to see the reassuring brass case in the chamber, and he could feel the weight of nine more cartridges in the magazine. He went silently up the first three steps, and knowing the next would give away his movement, he took the last three in one movement. He crouched below the window line, peering through the yellowed lace curtains, then moved into the living room, scanning the area with the front sight of the small pistol.

Coming into the entryway, he glanced out the frosted glass in the front door and saw the dark wavy outline of a man, standing back on the edge of the front porch. He settled the glowing orange gunsight on the largest part of the shadow, trying to decide if he should take a chance and open the door, or just punch a series of holes in whoever was standing on the opposite side.

Whoever they were, they weren't invited. No one should have known he was coming back to the family house, and he didn't think any of the neighbors would be coming for a visit. He pressed the gun forward with his right hand and squeezed back with his left to steady the shot.

"Mr. Diggs?" came a shout from the porch.

He remained silent and holding on target.

"Mr. Diggs, I'm here to hand-deliver a message. A time-critical message."

"A message from who?" Diggs responded, still keeping steady aim on the wavy shadow through the glass.

"He said to tell you it was from a tall handsome Russian. That you would understand."

In his many interactions with Eli Moskarov, Diggs had often referred to him as a "tall, handsome Russian," mostly just to annoy Eli. It became a joke of sorts within the intelligence community.

"How did the Russian know where to find me?"

"I couldn't answer that, sir. I was contacted this

morning and told where to find you and deliver an urgent communication. I'm supposed to let you read it, then retrieve and destroy it. That's all I'm privy to, sir."

Diggs released his left hand and reached down to open the door, keeping the pistol trained forward and his eyes never leaving the sweet spot on his sight picture. He opened the door swiftly and came out with the gun at chest level. The young man on the porch reflexively stepped back and nearly went off the edge.

He had a face like a ten-year-old, pale peachy skin, and dark hair slicked back with gel. He looked odd wearing a black suit and tie, like he was dressed up for an uncle's funeral. His hands were stretched out to each side, a folded and sealed piece of paper gripped tightly in the left.

"You're a little young to be a spy, aren't you?" Diggs said.

"I'm just part of the diplomatic corps at the Embassy, sir. Not a spy."

Diggs smiled for the second time today, "All Israeli diplomats are spies, boy. Hand me the message, and don't move too quickly. I'm old, and my shaky hands might set this gun off."

The young man looked nervously at the round hole on the end of the pistol, then slowly moved his hand forward with the folded paper. Diggs took it in his left hand, pried open the seal with his thumbnail, and unfolded it, the Glock still aiming forward. He glanced down and up in one-second intervals to read the note and keep an eye on the young Israeli.

" *Bill,*

The party you threw in Mallorca hasn't ended … moving to new location. Unexpected guests are arriving soon. Very dangerous situation that requires immediate intervention." Eli.

DIGGS' head began to spin at the implication of what he was reading. First, the Mossad had obviously been watching his movements, and knew about the assassinations in Mallorca. But how much did they know? And who were the unexpected guests?

Had the Fairhope Group and everyone involved been compromised, or just him?

"I was told that if you wanted to respond, it would be best for you to ride back with me to a safe house and use an encrypted line. They assumed you wouldn't want to be photographed anywhere near the Israel Embassy."

"They were right about that. Where is your safe house?"

"Williamsburg, Virginia. Just down the road from 'The Farm'," the young Israeli said. Then he added, "The safest place for spies, is as close to other spies as they can get."

13

WILLIAMSBURG, VIRGINIA

The Israeli safe house was an apartment above a country store on State Road 5, The Glen Rose General, just outside Williamsburg. They owned the store as well, and the nice old couple that ran it, Bud and Margaret, had been in the employ of the Israeli Intelligence Service for thirty-six years.

State Road 5 was the main travel route of people driving back and forth from Washington to the CIA training facility, Camp Peary, and company personnel frequently stopped in the little store to buy snacks and drinks for the road. They had no idea the Israelis in the room above were cataloging their photographs, monitoring their movements, conversations, and sometimes hacking into their cell phones with laser tags.

"I haven't been here in years," Diggs said as they

pulled into the driveway of the Glen Rose General. "They've got the best heat-lamp hotdogs in Virginia, and unlimited refills on fountain sodas."

"American spies are suckers for free refills," the young Israeli said.

"Wait. You're not telling me this is your safe house ... Bud and Margaret are watchers? That completely wrecks my sense of reality."

"Commander Moskarov thought this might be entertaining for you."

"That's why I always loved working with you guys. You never fail to surprise me."

They parked the car at the side of the building and walked around back to the stairs leading up to the flat. The apartment was very sparsely decorated. A sleeper sofa, a kitchenette, and a small round table with four plain wooden chairs. In the center of the table was a laptop computer, and an encrypted satellite telephone.

"They should be calling any moment, Mr. Diggs."

"They were sure I'd be arriving with you at a specific time? That's confident," Diggs replied.

"Oh, no sir. But I'm sure they watched us enter the flat, and they are watching us now."

The telephone rang a second later. The young Israeli agent gestured for Diggs to answer, as he went out the door, "I'll leave you to your call, sir."

Diggs punched the button for the speaker, "I'm

sure you have the room wired, Eli, so no need to hold the receiver to my ear."

"Hello old friend. After hearing that you had retired from the CIA last year, it came as a shock when we started seeing you popping up all over the Mediterranean, and a few places in the Gulf. But you never came to see me in Tel Aviv. I was heartbroken."

"We were never that close, Eli. I was just enjoying my time off and visiting places I never got to see when I was working."

"I never took you for a tourist, Bill, and after the bodies started piling up, I thought maybe you were doing some off-the-books wet work for the company. But that wasn't it at all, was it?"

"I haven't the faintest idea what you're talking about."

"I'm talking about the Fairhope Group. We know all about it."

"You don't know shit, Eli. You're fishing." He was right, the Israelis didn't know much about Fairhope yet. "Tell me what you think you know, and I'll tell you if you're getting warm."

"Honestly, I couldn't quite place how the Algerian Ambassador to Spain, Farouk Kateb, was connected to all of the other corpses, and we've been watching him for years. But then the wiretaps on our friends in Beirut started buzzing with activity. Seems all of the men who died a few months ago, and all within days of each other, were connected to highly profitable criminal enterprises, and the money trail led back to Hezbollah."

Diggs didn't respond.

"Come on, Bill, I must be getting warm. I can see your core temperature going up on the infrared sensors in the room." He let that sink in for a minute, then added, "In the spirit of openness, I'll also confess to having some help sorting this out."

"From who?"

"A very beautiful young Jewish girl came home to Israel a few months ago. She had quite a story to tell. Her name is Avigail."

"Shit. I knew I should have dumped her in the sea the minute I saw her."

"That's exactly where she was found, floating in the sea. By an Arab princess or something, by her account. They fished her out of the water, cared for her, then asked her where she wanted to go. The only place she could think of was where she was born, Tel Aviv."

Now Diggs was backed into a corner. Avigail had been Farouk Kateb's little spy in Monte Carlo. She had wormed her way into Lucas' heart, been a witness to murders, could identify both Lucas and Diggs, and connect them to the killings in Mallorca. And to top it off, she had set them up to be killed by Farouk's hitman, Abd al-Rahman.

He diverted the subject, "Your message was

cryptic, Eli. Tell me about the unexpected guests and dangerous situation."

"Apparently you missed someone in the financing operation, Bill. Someone very quickly picked up the pieces of Banco Baudin, and managing the money laundering for enterprises linked to our enemies in Lebanon and Iran. They barely skipped a beat. And now, they are about to manage the assets for an alliance between the Islamic Jihadis, and the government-run cartels in the Caribbean."

"That sounds like government work, Eli. I'm a private citizen now."

"You might be private now, Bill, but some of your loose ends are coming home to roost. There's a new Cuban DI operative who's working in your old neighborhood, Caracas. His name is Raphael Ortega, and he's the one who put this deal together.

The Iranians and Hezbollah have been cornering the opium trade, but a kilo of opium that used to be worth twenty thousand dollars on the street, is now only worth about three hundred. The Chinese and their synthetic opioids have decimated their market value.

They are trying to put together a synthetic lab operation in Venezuela with help from the Russians, and create pills from a fentanyl-like chemical mixed with their opium. That would convert every kilo of pure opium into twenty-million dollars' worth of pills. All they lack is a reliable smuggling and distribution chain into the United States, but we think they have that worked out now.

Besides splitting the money from drugs sales, the cartels in South America that are linked to the Venezuelan government will gain a new outlet for trafficking young women, because the mullahs are constantly looking for new flesh."

"Where did you get this intel, Eli?"

"The bulk of the story came from Avigail. Seems she was sitting in the room when the initial discussions were taking place last year. Farouk Kateb really trusted her, and her old boss at Banco Baudin was a pillow talker. We've been monitoring all the players for several months, and it checked out. But now it's happening, and happening fast. The handshakes and money transfers are going down in Curaçao in twelve days."

"What do you have in mind, Eli?"

"Israel will not allow Hezbollah to reach across the ocean and develop a partnership with the cartels or the Cuban DI, and find a new source of money to wage war on Jews. We've been able to identify the emissary, and we need to make sure he doesn't complete that mission. We will either find a creative way to intervene, or we'll just take him out. But I can't justify taking direct action in the Caribe on Cubans or others who aren't officially enemies of Israel. The banker from Gibraltar is someone I know you and your partners in the Fairhope Group are interested in."

"Who is the banker, and why is he of any interest to us?"

"Because he's rebuilding the network of human-traffickers and drug dealers that you took out of action just a few months ago. He popped up on our radar last month when we were monitoring communications between some of Hezbollah's people in Lebanon and a cell in Morocco. I've had eyes and ears on him ever since."

Diggs thought for a moment before answering, "Do you have any real intel on him? What's his name? Where is he from? Who has he been seen with? Do you have any photographs?"

"He keeps an office in his home on Gibraltar. He doesn't have banking offices, so we think he is completely off the books. Goes by the name of Constantino Gallo, but we're still trying to reference that through the system. So far nothing, so it's likely an alias. He went dark before we could put a tracker on him after the last conversation with his handler in Beirut. We had audio surveillance, but we weren't in a position to take him off the street. I'll see if there are any known photos, and let you know.

"We would have to wait until the banker shows himself for the meeting with the emissary in Curaçao before we can take him. Do you have a plan?"

"Yes. Replace the emissary before the meet. As far

as we can tell from the communications, the banker and the emissary, Aziz Harrak, have never met. They know of each other, but never been in the same room. Aziz is being left to coordinate his own travel and delivery system, and it's not likely anyone in Curaçao will know him either, because he hasn't traveled outside of North Africa and Spain. Who would know if we made a last minute substitution?

We'll need a man who can pass for Mediterranean in complexion, close to thirty years old, and speaks both Spanish and French-Arabic natively. It would help if he's well trained. Know anyone who fits that description?"

"In point of fact, I do."

"The plan will have a better chance of success if we can gain control of as many of the logistical issues as possible. Since this opportunity was just passed on to Aziz, I'm sure he's trying to come up with his own plans to safely transport a billion dollars' worth of opium across the ocean."

"I might have an option we can lay in front of him for that dilemma as well. Let me make a few calls, and I'll give you confirmation one way or the other before I get on my flight this afternoon at La Guardia."

"This needs a quick, mobile response, Bill. The kind of thing you and Lucas Martell seem to be very adept at. And I don't want to hand this over to an ass-kisser like Mathew Penn in Caracas. Then I'd have to tell the CIA where all of my intel came from, and I don't think you want me to do that."

"Were you listening to my calls?"

"Of course not, you're my friend. I was listening to Mathew's calls."

That didn't make Diggs feel any better about being pressed into service for the Israeli Mossad. And now he had to tell Lucas and Eliza that they were also compromised.

Then, as if he read his mind, Eli said, "Bill, I swear to you as a friend, nothing about you, Lucas, or the Fairhope Group will leak from me or my office."

Diggs stared out the front window of the small apartment, across the rolling pines and swamp forest beyond. There were young men and women out there somewhere, being trained and conditioned for service in the clandestine division of the Central Intelligence Agency. Just like he had been over forty years ago. He wondered if anything he had ever done for the CIA had really made a difference in the world. The lies. The crimes. The interrogations and murders.

"I'll have my embassy attaché drive you to Central Station in D.C., and he'll give you a burner phone with a message line programmed into speed dial. When you arrive in Caracas, I can arrange for support there too, if needed."

"I didn't think Israel had any diplomatic staff or offices in Venezuela?"

"Officially, we don't."

"I noticed on the door downstairs in the general store, that you have Free Wi-Fi. Do you mind if I use an encrypted device to send a message?"

"Be my guest."

DIGGS CONNECTED his laptop to the internet through a 256-bit encrypted VPN, then signed into a further encrypted private messaging server. The server was located in the Seychelles Islands, in the Indian Ocean, the virtual hub of the Fairhope Group.

There were only two other people in the world who had access to the messaging. He addressed the communications to both.

"*Traveling to Caracas to investigate an incident. Urgent conference required.*"

14

THE ISLAND KINGDOM OF MALADH, GULF OF ARABIA

In the Persian Gulf, nestled off the coast of the United Arab Emirates, between Qatar and Dubai, is a nearly unknown little kingdom. A group of three islands, only one of which is large enough to hold a city, and that city is still surrounded by the original mud-stone walls stretching to the high dunes that have held back the sea since they receded after the great flood. Although now, they are only a facade, a relic of what once was.

The island was one of the first places that men took refuge and began again, after God wiped the earth clean. It was a sanctuary that offered natural sweet-water wells, fat date palms for sustenance and shade, and enough grasses and prickly shrubs grew on the island to keep a few small herds of goats.

There were two sheltered coves to harbor small

boats for fishing, and the deep azure waters were abundant. It was a haven, and so aptly given the same name in the old Arabic tongue, Maladh.

The island of Maladh has been ruled by Sultans from the same family for the last six-hundred years, and the kingdom had only limited contact with the outside world until the 1950's. In 1961, just one year after neighboring Qatar's first offshore oil discovery was made, the Sultan allowed a French oil company to test-drill just off the main cove, where he could personally keep watch on their doings from his mud-brick castle perched on the hill.

Within the next twenty years, the territorial waters surrounding the islands had six drilling platforms in full operation, and there was a small refinery and deep-water loading cay on one of the smaller, uninhabited islets. Tanker ships came weekly to cart away the oil to distant lands. The Sultan of Maladh was worth more money than he, or the next five generations that came from his blood, could ever spend.

Maladh has only thirty-thousand native residents, but the Sultan showered his people with wealth, and the city flourished. Streets were paved, stores and high-rise apartment buildings replaced the mud shacks, and now the deep water coves are home to mega-yachts. But beneath the shiny modern-world surface, some of the old ways still linger.

It was hot today. A scalding, desiccating heat. The kind of heat that snuffs out life from any who wander too far from shade. The black asphalt of the city street was shimmering, as if on the verge of reverting back to liquid. The sound of Michelin tires rolling over the sticky surface was reminiscent of Velcro being pulled apart, as a champagne silver Rolls Royce Phantom eased to a stop in front of the Golden Dove Cafe.

Four men were huddled around an iron table with a thick rose-marble top, beneath the broad shadow of a brilliant blue canopy. To a stranger, they would have been difficult to tell apart. All wearing traditional white bisht robes, and black and white patterned shemaghs wound around their heads. They all had salt-and-pepper beards that hid the distinguishing features of the face, and the only thing that demonstrated any animation of life were the thick black eyebrows that arched and squinted as they spoke.

They were older men. Old enough to remember this place long before the streets were paved and the buildings were taller than the palm trees. Old enough to remember when this was an outdoor fruit market with dirt floors and walls made of hand-shaped mud. And before the sidewalk beneath them was made of imported Egyptian granite.

As they sat in the shade and sipped karak-chai tea

from gold inlaid cups, they bitched and moaned, lamenting the disappearance of the old ways, a simple herdsman's life, and traditional Islam. None of them had had to work for over forty years, as the old Sultan had spread great wealth to his flock, but still, they lamented. And now they had something new to groan about. The new young Sultan, and his love of modern things and western ways.

As the silver Phantom came to a stop, they all paused from conversation and stared, tea cups suspended in front of their mouths. The front passenger side door opened, and a tall broad shouldered man stepped out. He was not wearing traditional Arab clothing, but a black, tailored suit. He wore a short cut beard as dark as his clothing, and black Ray-Ban sunglasses. He stood motionless for a moment, looking purposefully in all directions. Then the driver stepped out, his twin in size and dress, exiting the car and looking in the opposite direction.

Convinced there was no threat to his charge, the passenger-side guard opened the rear door and offered his hand to assist her. The woman's jeweled shoes sparkled in the sunlight as she reached out for the granite walkway with long legs. Her dress was sufficiently long to shield them from view, but as they stretched out, the creamy flesh of her ankles was exposed for an instant.

The bushy eyebrows of the old men flicked and squinted in disapproval.

Her hand accepted the one offered by her guard, and she stood up from the car, nearly as tall as he was, but slender and shapely beneath the saffron colored silk dress. Her head was covered with a gold embroidered scarf that wrapped around, and left only her eyes and the hints of perfect cheek bones visible to the world.

It was the eyes that gave her identity away, the color of Indian tourmaline.

"Abaasa," one of the old men muttered as the woman and her guards passed.

As she heard him speak, the woman paused before entering the cafe. The two guards needed no direction. They pivoted and lunged at the old men.

Four tea cups crashed to the table as the men reeled from their chairs and flung themselves prostrate onto the granite sidewalk. They lay there, face down with the hot stone sizzling their flesh, but terrified to move. The one who had uttered the word, quickly pleaded, "Mercy, mercy!"

The woman looked at the men and enjoyed a few seconds of their suffering on the burning hot surface, then she gently nodded to the guards.

One guard leaned over the old men and whispered, "You have lived from the infinite well of the Sultan, but today you continue living by the mercy of Sultana," he said.

The old men quivered and whimpered, but did not speak another word, nor raise their faces until the woman and her guards had entered the cafe and were out of sight.

~

"ABAASA" was the name given to her as a child, and she despised it. It means, "Lioness," and indeed, when she was first abducted from her family's home in Mallorca, Spain at the age of eleven, and caged like an animal for transport into a life of slavery, she rained hell on anyone who came near her, with slashing claws and gnashing teeth. Her given name, was Eliza Martell.

Twelve years ago, at the direction of an Algerian crime lord, Farouk Kateb, Eliza was snatched from her doorstep by a band of Moroccan henchmen. She was delivered to Farouk, and he in turn used her as a gift to gain favor with the Sultan of Maladh.

The old Sultan had put out the call to search for the rarest of jewels, to begin building a harem for his only son, Hassan. Eliza was arguably one of the most beautiful young girls in the Mediterranean. Olive Spanish skin, long golden hair that flowed in the wind, and jewel-green eyes. She was the only daughter of a business associate of Farouk. He had seen her by chance one day at her father's office and knew instantly that she was worth a fortune in favors from the Sultan of Maladh. Farouk was a professional in the fulfillment of vile desires, among many other things.

The son of the Sultan was only twelve at the time, but it was thought he could become accustomed to the female company first and explore his desires as they developed naturally. He was enamored with his new playmate from the moment he laid eyes on her. Eliza looked nothing like any other young girl he had ever seen, for he had only known the locals of Maladh, who all had dark hair and brown eyes.

"She has hair like the golden lions of the desert that grandfather told me stories about. I want to call her 'Abaasa'," he told his father, the Sultan.

"She belongs to you. You may call her anything you wish. But she does not speak our language and she is a very wild creature. You will have to train her," his father answered.

The boy was being raised in a world of wealth and privilege beyond the imagination of mortal men. To him, the concept of owning slaves was normal, but he had no understanding of where they came from.

He didn't know that Eliza had been a happy child with a loving family, until she was ripped away from her life to become a gift for him. Indeed, at his age, he had very little understanding of the world outside his little island kingdom, and no understanding at all of the way other people lived. In his mind, all the world existed only to serve his father, and someday himself.

But the boy was not without a kind heart, and as

he grew, and as he and Eliza learned to communicate, he fell deeply in love with her. And even though his harem grew in the years leading up to his age of ascension, he would never love another the way he loved the girl with hair of gold, his Abaasa.

THEN ONE DAY, the old Sultan died, and the boy, now twenty-three, became the new Sultan of Maladh. He would have many official wives in the years to come, but the one he loved most he could never marry under the old laws of Islam, because she was not of this land nor a true believer in the prophet. Instead, the young Sultan gifted Eliza with the title of "Chief Consort to the Sultan", and in doing so, made her one of the most powerful women in the Persian Gulf.

In some ways, Eliza had come to love Hassan. He was kind to her, generous beyond belief, and in the few years since he ascended to the throne of Maladh, he had allowed her freedoms that no woman bound in slavery to a Sultan could ever have imagined.

She was allowed to roam not only the island kingdom, but the world at will. With her personal guards at her side, she had access to his private jets, yachts, and fortunes. He had known her for most of his life, and he trusted her. As Chief Consort, she was not bound by the same rules that confined official wives, and she frequently served him in ways beyond the needs of the flesh.

She gained access to many of the darkest secrets of the Middle East. Eliza accompanied Hassan on most of his travels, and she developed a talent for hovering in the periphery as he met with his financiers, business partners, and frequently with leaders of other Muslim nations.

It was her responsibility to be invisible when he did not want her seen, and immediately available when he did, to wield her charms and beauty.

She took no offense to the role. Indeed, she realized very quickly that the tides had turned in her favor. Eliza bore no particular ill will toward Hassan. In some ways she truly loved him. But she had never forgotten that she once had another life. A life that was stolen from her, and regardless of the opulence in which she lived, and the freedoms the young Sultan allowed her, she was still a slave.

THE FIRST OF her two loyal guards, Mohammed, opened the elegant wood door to the Golden Dove, made a brief inspection of the occupants and staff inside, then nodded to Abdul, his partner. Adbul held the door open for Eliza and watched the street behind her, as Mohammed entered and took up a position near two doors on the back wall. One door led to the kitchen. The other to a private room.

The owner of the cafe, a middle-aged man with oddly pale flesh, a graying beard, and dressed in a golden kafka, rushed to greet Eliza as she entered. He paused far in front of her, and leaned faintly forward, as he touch his forehead with his fingertips, "Sultana, 'As-salaam alaykum' (peace be upon you)."

"Wa alaykum as-salaam," she returned.

"You bless us with your presence. Your private space is waiting. May I offer you karak-chai tea? It is very fresh, and most excellent today."

"No, thank you."

The owner stepped aside, and Eliza moved to the back where Mohammed was now holding open the door to the private room. She moved with such grace, that without being able to see her feet beneath the long dress, she appeared to float across the room.

The private room was square, with a tall ceiling painted in gold leaf, and the walls paneled in Turkish walnut. The floor was a green-flecked marble, and in the center of the room was a white granite table. Mohammed pulled a small wand-shaped instrument from inside his jacket, pressed a button on the end, and began to sweep the perimeter to detect any electronic listening devices. He finished by waving the wand over, under, and around the table, "The room is secure, Sultana," he said.

Abdul removed a very compact tablet from a

metal case that he had carried from the car. He laid it on the table, then pulled a chair away and attended while Eliza landed softly on the cushioned seat and pulled it close.

"Thank you. May I have a few moments alone, please," she said. Despite the fact that both men were guardians and servants to her every whim, she had always treated Mohammed and Abdul in a way that endeared her to them. They believed her to be an angel, sent from God himself, and they would die for her without question or hesitation.

"As you wish, Sultana. We will be only a step away."

As they left, she turned the tablet on, held it in front of her for the facial recognition scanner to allow entry, then connected to a highly secured wi-fi router that was concealed within the front wall of the room. Only she knew it even existed, and only she had the passcodes to connect to it. She used a special secured program to access the internet, then entered the codes to access yet another private server. One that lay deep within the protected walls of a private bank in the Seychelles Islands, in the Indian Ocean.

Eliza had secretly funded the building of the Golden Dove Cafe, and the private electronic communications network was her secret connection to the rest of the world when she was on the island of Maladh. Courtesy of Bill Diggs and a few of his old friends from the National Reconnaissance Office.

As she signed into the message board, an alert popped up:

**Urgent Communications Request. Join Audio Conference in Progress?*

She pulled an earpiece from her handbag and twisted it lightly into her right ear, then entered, YES.

15

_participant has joined the conference_* Flashed up on the monitors of both Lucas and Diggs' computers.

LUCAS WELCOMED his sister to the conversation. "Hello, glad you could join us."

Diggs resumed what he had just started explaining to Lucas, "A significant threat has just been brought to my attention, with request for intervention.

An old friend of mine in Tel Aviv just went to a great deal of trouble to contact me.

"Is your old friend Mossad?" Eliza asked.

"Yes. They have uncovered an event going down in Curaçao, just off the coast of Venezuela, in twelve days. It involves a known associate of our old friend,

Farouk Kateb, who is moving up the chain of command with the enemies of Israel."

Eliza spoke again, "Our mission doesn't directly involve action to protect the Israelis. Why would he contact you? And for that matter, why would he think you could do anything to help him? You're supposed to be retired from the CIA."

"The Mossad has been monitoring anyone involved with the jihadis or working to finance the jihadis, for many years. The banker in Monte Carlo and Farouk had become primary targets, and they were monitoring them very closely. Naturally, they were quite stunned when we eliminated everyone on their own hit list. They were grateful, but curious. These people are very good at what they do, so eventually they would have put it together, but, they had an additional informant … Avigail."

"Avi is working with the Mossad, now?' Lucas asked.

"Apparently she's renewing her bonds with her Jewish heritage."

Eliza spoke, "Neither one of you are qualified to judge her. She's been through things you couldn't imagine."

"Yes, you're right. My apologies. Eli said she had been very generous with information from her old life, including what she had heard about the event unfolding in twelve days. And, I'm sure she filled in a few details about us. They don't know everything, but they know about me and Lucas, and that we are part of the Fairhope Group. They don't know exactly what our mission is, yet."

"What's the event in Curaçao?" Lucas asked.

"An alliance is being brokered between the Arabs and the Venezuelans. An emissary connected to Hezbollah is meeting with a Cuban DI operative, who's representing the Venezuelans. The Iranians are looking for a South American partner to produce a drug in pill form, combining their opium with synthetic fentanyl. They also need the South Americans to set up a reliable supply chain into the United States."

Eliza responded again, "I understand why the Israelis wouldn't want Iran and their Hezbollah proxies to get their hands on more money, but again, this is outside the scope of why the Fairhope Group was formed."

"Yes, but they are also establishing a back-channel distribution for human-trafficking from South America to the Middle East. The cartels will increase the number of young girls they kidnap and traffic by many thousands, with the larger guaranteed market to the mullahs."

"That's a different story. I'll agree to take action if you think it's warranted," Eliza said.

"There's one more piece of interesting information. It seems that immediately after we retired the bad-actors in Monte Carlo and Mallorca, someone else stepped in very quickly and took over the management of the accounts and assets for our entire target list. The banker wasn't dead more than a day before he had been replaced, and the new banker is taking orders directly from Beirut.

"Do you know who it is?" Lucas asked.

"The only name I have to work with at the moment is Constantino Gallo, but that is definitely an alias. Whoever he is, he's going to be there on site in Curaçao. It might be our only opportunity to gain access to some of the information we've been missing. It's a rare opportunity to catch one of bankers away from their own security caves. We might be able to take him alive."

"I'm in," Lucas said.

"You might want to let me give you the rough outline suggested by the Mossad, before you agree. The plan they suggested, and I can't think of anything better, is to snatch the emissary after he's arrived in Curaçao, and replace him with our own operative. You just happen to be a perfect fit."

"I'm still in. I'm in this all the way, no matter what it takes."

"I'm sure you can handle it, Lucas, or I wouldn't suggest it, but this is beyond the scope of anything you've faced before. The Cuban DI operatives are some of the best in the world, and they are lethal. We won't have time to train for this. It's going to be fluid, and you'll have to adapt on the fly."

"It's no different than the operation in Mallorca, Diggs."

"Yes, and that nearly ended up with you and the Frenchman dead. Speaking of that, can you bring Serge on board? We'll be going in with no other backup, and he's an outstanding sniper."

"I'll contact him now, but I'm sure he's a go."

"Good. Make those arrangements now, and be ready to go within twenty-four hours.

I received a call early this morning from the CIA Station Chief in Caracas, alerting me about another incident involving a bombing, and possible links to current abduction cases. I don't know yet, but I wonder if they might be connected with the deal in Curaçao. I'm enroute now, and I'll know more by this time tomorrow afternoon.

Eliza, I'm going to send you a separate file with some logistical needs."

"I'll be waiting. Whatever you need, I'll see to it."

Lucas waited until both Eliza and Diggs had logged off the network, then he shut his connection down as well. He gingerly raised a cup to his lips and took another sip of hot coffee. Then his mind drifted to the endless lists of numbered accounts, in banks around the world, that he'd taken from Jean Étienne Berger, the piece-of-garbage President of Banco Baudin in Monaco. Make that, ex-President.

Accounts that belonged to the most evil and corrupt men across the Mediterranean, Middle East, and Africa. Likely many others as well, who lived in no particular place, but migrated here and there to keep their tracks well hidden.

After finishing his coffee, he stood and walked to the terrace balustrade, took one extended glance at the beautiful women who were beginning to stretch out over the sand on colorful towels, then went into the house, to his father's old summer office.

Lucas' father, Francisco, had been a senior executive of Banco Baudin, and worked with most of their wealthiest clients in the Middle East. It was his sudden death in a car accident in Monaco that brought Lucas back home, and ultimately to discover that his old boss, Berger, was involved with the human-trafficking operations that had kidnapped Eliza.

From the day Eliza was taken, Lucas and his father had barely spoken. Francisco Martell had withdrawn into his work, traveled often, and drank heavily when he was home. What remained of their family fell apart. Lucas' mother took a large quantity of sleeping pills and slipped into the bathtub. Francisco slipped away from his duties as a father.

Lucas went back into the house, to his study, and pulled up a carpet to expose his hidden safe in the floor. He spun the dial quickly back and forth and pulled open the steel door. It contained only two things; the encrypted pen-drive with all of the information he'd acquired from Banco Baudin, and a compact Walther pistol. He was only interested in the drive at the moment.

He sat at the small mahogany desk, plugged the drive into his computer, and opened the files. He wasn't quite sure what he was looking for. Maybe a pattern or clue about the identity of the account owners or locations. He wondered if any of the accounts might be in Venezuela, given Diggs' sudden departure.

It was like trying to read Albert Einstein's mathematical formulas. Routing codes, account numbers and user codenames. Since most of these were accessed via the internet, they were all assigned international (ISO) codes to regulate digital access. He had the keys to finding all of Fairhope Group's targets in his hand, but it was going to take some specialized talent to sift through it.

16

TEL AVIV, ISRAEL

Eli Moskarov gazed out the rear window of the BMW sedan as it passed through the congested streets of Tel Aviv, then into the open desert hills beyond. He gave little notice to the scattered olive groves and orange trees that were springing up along the edge of the lands reclaimed decades ago from the Palestinians, and now flourishing under the till of young Jewish families. He was preoccupied with the conversation he was about to have with a beautiful young woman.

Avigail is a very old Hebrew name, and even though she was born in Tel Aviv, she could hardly be considered a dedicated Jew. Born to an Israeli mother and an Algerian father, she was a child of mixed heritage, and opposing loyalties. Her early years were spent growing up happily in Tel Aviv, but her father was not a benevolent man or a good husband, and when she was only eight, he snatched Avigail and her younger sister and fled across the border into Algeria.

His original intention was to extort his wife's family for ransom to return his daughters, but instead, he decided to simply sell them into the human-slavery market in Algiers.

Avigail was thrust into a hell beyond the comprehension of most people, but she survived. At the age of fourteen, she was noticed and "rescued" to some extent, by the nefarious criminal, Farouk Kateb. He raised her, educated her, trained her in the arts of deception and seduction, and transformed her into the perfect female operative for a criminal mastermind.

Now at the age of thirty two, she was the epitome of a Mediterranean beauty. She had a silky brown complexion like sun-dried olives, long black hair that cascaded in waves to her rounded hips, and eyes that defied any attempt to chart their true color. In the morning light, they took the color of the soft green sea, and in the afternoon, they turned to a gray that mirrored the late day storms.

Avigail was extremely intelligent, and spoke Hebrew, Spanish, Arabic, French, and English with equal skill. She was highly intuitive when it came to manipulating the fantasies of men to her advantage; mysterious, alluring in motion, and cool under stress.

But her life was recently turned completely upside down. Farouk had kept her based in Monte Carlo, carefully watching and manipulating the banker who managed all of his illicit corporate assets. Until Lucas Martell came into the picture.

Avigail had fallen unexpectedly and inexplicably in love. And yet, she still did as her master had commanded of her, and led Lucas and his partners to what should have been a certain death at the hands of his assassins.

In her worst moment aboard the yacht of Farouk Kateb in the open sea, her betrayal of the man she loved seized her, and she threw herself into the crashing waves to die. But, it seems, it wasn't her time. She was pulled from the water by someone who had pity on her, and gave her a choice, "Where would like to go?" The only place she could think of was the place she had spent her only happy years, Tel Aviv, Israel.

Mother Israel, and the Mossad in particular, welcomed Avigail home. She had knowledge of the North African criminal underworld and financial enterprises that benefited Israel's most lethal enemies. She was a treasure trove of information, and she willingly shared what she knew.

All she really wanted at that time was to find herself. To learn who she could have been, and might still be. Her family had all passed away, but Eli Moskarov comforted her, in his own way, as a spy master.

Eli saw the strength and sophistication that she possessed, as well as the fact that she had seen and done things, and been more deeply imbedded in the workings of the Arab world than any other "walk-in" he had ever encountered. And he intended to use her when it best suited him.

THEY HAD BEEN DRIVING for half an hour down a dusty road in what seemed like the middle of nowhere. A place where only the lost, or those who wish not to be found, would go. Then, a brilliant green valley appeared as they crested a hill. A small, agricultural oasis in a sea of sand. The perfect place to hide a Mossad training camp. The bodyguard driving Eli's car turned around in his seat, "We're here sir. I can see her walking in the garden to the right."

"Just stop here, I'll walk out to her," Eli said.

He waited a few moments when the car stopped, for the dust to blow away, before he opened the door and stepped out. Looking out over the grove of oranges and nectarines, he could see her standing with her hand shielding the sun from her eyes and watching him walk towards her. She smiled and waved.

Avigail was adapting to her roots. She wore cool linen pants and a simple white blouse to ward off the heat, and her hair was tied back in a spiral knot, which it never would have been in her previous life, and wrapped with a turquoise cloth. She no longer looked the part of the Muslim spy, but of a modest Jewish girl who lived in the valley.

Eli embraced her warmly, "Hello, Avi. I'm sorry I haven't come to see you in so long."

"That's alright, Eli. I'm quite happy here. It's peaceful and quiet, and I'm finally able to sleep almost through the nights now."

"Your instructors have told me, and they say you've been very helpful."

"I want to be helpful. I want Israel to be my home, and I want to be a part of this place. I've never really belonged anywhere."

"I'm happy to hear that. Let's walk, shall we. I have something to discuss with you that relates precisely to that subject," he said. Then he reached out his hand as a father would take his daughter's, and they walked along through the fragrant fruit trees.

They walked for several minutes in silence before he spoke, "I know you are still adjusting to your new life, Avi, and I hate to approach you with a request to help Israel so soon, but something is happening that only you are truly capable of dealing with."

She stopped and let go of his hand. She knew this day would come. The day when Eli and Israel would begin to demand she repay their generosity, just as Farouk Kateb had demanded of her, but it was too soon. "Eli, please. I can't. Don't make me go back to that world. I'll tell you anything you want to know about those people, but don't send me back!"

"I know, Avi. I know it's too soon, and I would never have wanted to ask this, but it's not just for me. There is someone else involved, and only your presence might keep him alive. It's someone you care about."

"I don't have anyone in this world I care about, Eli. I know you've been kind to me, but I don't even care enough about you to go back there."

"Do you care enough about Lucas Martell?"

The name rolling off his lips struck her down like a hammer blow. He could see her knees falter, and her eyes dropped to the ground in shame. Eli knew it was as low a blow as he could strike to coerce her, but it was his only play.

"Tell me what you want," she said without ever looking up to meet his eyes.

"In your past life, did you ever encounter a young man named Aziz, in Marrakesh?"

"Yes, I know Aziz. He's a wormy little Spanish shit who fancies himself a jihad warrior. He was one of Farouk's lapdogs."

"Well, Aziz is now a man of position within Hezbollah's business organization. And he has just been given a special mission to act as an emissary for them in a meeting in the Caribbean. We intend to remove Aziz, and replace him with someone else - Lucas Martell."

"Why would Lucas be interested in working with you?"

"He has his reasons."

"What do you want from me?"

"We need someone who can get close to Aziz and help us intercept him at a point beyond the sight of his people. My team will take him, and Lucas will take his place. Then, if you're willing to do this, you will accompany Lucas to Curaçao and pose as his assistant and translator."

"I don't know if I'm ready to face Lucas, Eli. He must despise me. He probably wants me dead. I betrayed him," she said.

I have it on good account that he doesn't hate you. And he has his own personal mission to attend to that will keep him focused. But if you won't help us capture Aziz out of the view of his Hezbollah handlers, then I'll just have to kill him before he leaves Morocco, and Lucas will be on his own."

Avigail looked up and turned to the north, and from the hills where they stood, she could see the Mediterranean Sea and the white caps breaking ahead of a western wind. She was searching in her mind for a place beyond where she could see, two hundred miles further to the island of Mallorca. To the place where she felt real love for the first time.

"Do you have a plan for me to reappear in Morocco after all this time? These men live in a world of paranoia. They suspect everyone they meet, and believe everyone they haven't seen in a while is an Israeli spy."

"Farouk had a smuggling associate in Barcelona, a Belgian business man. Did you know him?"

"Yes, Gregor. I met him several times."

"We'll arrange to get a message to him that you were seen there in the Arab Quarter, and then he will likely find you. You should be able to convince him to get you into Morocco, then make your way to Aziz. You already have a very plausible story, from the murder of Jean-Étiene Berger in Monte Carlo, to leaving Mallorca with Farouk and then being picked up in the sea.

Telling a facsimile of the truth is the easy way to keep your story consistent. The only part you'll have to embellish is where you've been for the past few months, and we can create some check points for Aziz to verify your tracks if he wants to. I suspect that after Aziz sees you, his interest in revealing you for a spy will be far from the front of his mind."

"Are you telling me to sleep with him? Is that what you want from me, Eli?"

"I'm telling you to do what's needed to stay alive and accomplish the mission. You've done this for a living before Avi, you can handle it."

"All this time I thought you might be a kind man,

Eli. But you're just a bastard like all the rest. You'll use me and throw me away when I can't help you anymore."

"I use every resource I have to keep my people safe, Avi. And whether you believe it or not, you are one of my people. I care about your safety, but none of us have any pride left to worry about. What we do is about survival for all Israelis."

AVIGAIL SPENT THAT NIGHT SLEEPLESS, staring at the shapes and shadows that flickered in through the window, and thinking about Lucas. How could she face him after what she had done? How does a woman tell a man that she loves him, after she left him to be murdered? She realized now that years of conditioning had brainwashed her to do anything Farouk Kateb demanded of her, but still, how could she explain that to him.

He might never accept her explanation. He might reject her and scorn her, but at least if she did this one thing, it might repay a small portion of the debt she owed to him.

17

MARRAKESH, MOROCCO

Aziz Harrak rarely walked through the souk market-places in the Medina, the old walled city-within-a-city in Marrakesh. He despised the westerners and British tourists who permeated the old world with their foul culture. Young women dressed like whores, and pale-skinned European men sneered at the local Moroccans who struggled for life every day. He'd considered many times, the ways he could murder thousands in a single sweep, but it would cost too many lives of his people with them.

He considered the Moroccans his people, even though he was born and raised in Granada, Spain. Many generations of his family before him were also born in Granada and lived the entirety of their lives in the old Moorish quarter, the Albayzín. It was a counterfeit of old Morocco. A twisting labyrinth of brick streets and alleyways, and busy markets that resembled the souks of Marrakesh. Popular with the tourists, but they were not really souks. Nor were the occupants and merchants any longer real Moroccans.

His given name was Ferdinand Harrak. It always seemed an offense to him that his parents named him for the ancient king of Spain and attached it to his proud Arabic surname. He grew up speaking Spanish as his first language, and had to prod his parents into teaching him the foundations of Arabic at night.

By the time he was fifteen, he knew the truth. That he would always be poor, and as long as he lived in the Albayzín he would never be anything more than an amusing attraction to people with money. Like the monkey-boy in a traveling circus, wearing a funny fez cap and begging for change.

Ferdinand Harrak was a ripe target for recruiting.

He discovered that selling drugs to the tourists, in particular to the British and the Belgians, was much easier money than trying to sell scarfs or pottery. He started with small stuff first, pot and hash. After a time, his clientele changed, and the demand for opium forced him to consider expanding his business. But opium was more difficult for a smalltime street seller to acquire, and he didn't want to become a thug for a bigger dealer. He wanted to be the bigger dealer.

And that's when he landed in jail for the first time,

at seventeen. Ensnared in a Spanish police bust, he was arrested and then released to his parents. His father, fearing for his future, decided perhaps a change of scenery would do the boy good. Maybe someplace, where life was even tougher than the Albayzín, would teach him to appreciate what he had. He sent him on a fishing boat across the Strait of Gibraltar, to live with a distant relative in Marrakesh, Morocco.

Within two months, he discarded the shameful name - Ferdinand - and took the name Aziz. He never returned to Spain. He did, however, maintain his friendships and contacts in Granada in the illicit drug trade, and found a way to prosper as a middleman.

In 2006 he met the man who would change his life and change his fortunes, Farouk Kateb.

Farouk Kateb, if that was his real name, was like a walking god to a boy like Aziz. As the story went, Farouk had grown up in Palestine, and escaped into Egypt when he was young. He made his way to Algeria, scraping for a living, until he came into the employ of a very prosperous smuggler in Algiers. He watched, he learned, he heeded every command of his employer. Until the day he decided to kill him and seize control of the business for himself.

He started out with several profitable opium smuggling routes, by way of camels across the open deserts, then moving the drugs into Spain on fishing vessels. He added human-trafficking to his operations before anyone realized there was such a thing, and he grew an empire worth many billions of dollars.

As he began to roll in money, he also rolled with the rich and famous of the Arab world in North Africa, including some lavish parties with the Prime Minister of Algeria. Then, as his influence grew, fortune smiled on him further. He was named as the first official Ambassador of Algeria to Spain.

Farouk Kateb had been given the diplomatic keys to the kingdom of free travel, crime, and laundering assets.

He also maintained his roots, in his hatred for the Israelis for their constant assault on Palestine, and in his support of holy jihad. In recent years, it became known that Farouk's largest business partners were based in Lebanon (Hezbollah) and Iran. Hezbollah needed funds to wage war against the infidels and to ultimately drive the Israelis into the sea, and Iran was their major supporter.

In unison, they had secretly been taking control of the opium production across central Arabia and North Africa. But it wasn't until their alliance with Farouk Kateb, that they gained the means to effectively deliver it to market.

Farouk had also introduced his new partners to

the highly profitable human-trafficking business. But all of this was a moot point now, as Farouk had completely disappeared several months ago. It was assumed he was dead, probably at the hands of an Israeli assassin, but no one knew for sure.

FAROUK HAD BROUGHT young Aziz under his wing, and eventually put him in control of all the distribution and smuggling operations between Morocco and Spain, the primary channel of drugs flowing into Europe, and abducted children flowing back to North Africa.

Aziz had become a very wealthy young man in his own right. He lived in a palace-like home outside the old city, in the modern district of Ville Nouvelle. It was designed in classic Moorish style, with pointed arches and stone terraces, two courtyards with tiled fountains, and surrounded by gardens of date palms and manicured orange trees. He was no longer poor and would never kneel to another westerner.

Farouk had also instilled in his young ward, the fire of Islam. Aziz did everything he could to assist his brothers in Palestine and Lebanon in their holy war, and he had wept many nights after word reached him that Farouk was likely murdered. When the business partners from Hezbollah came calling for his support, he vowed all that he had to the jihad.

The man that Aziz now took orders from was in Beirut, and four days ago he had contacted him with an urgent request. An emissary was needed to conclude a critical new alliance on the other side of the Atlantic Ocean. An alliance that would provide money for Palestine, Hezbollah, and the Muslim masters in Iran to finish the war against the Israelis. And at the same time, it would provide fresh merchandise for the flesh bazaars across the Middle East and the Mediterranean.

The agreement was largely done at this point, the negotiations having been completed by Aziz's predecessor, Farouk Kateb, but his assassination had stalled the process and caused the new allies in the Caribbean to have some nervous doubts about the partnership.

Aziz's responsibility was to safely arrive in Curaçao in the old Dutch Antilles with a large delivery of opium. Then he would verify the guaranteed deposit of $1.2 billion dollars into a bank account set up for this purpose. The leaders of Hezbollah were sending their official banker from Gibraltar to meet him at the bank, to support his verification of the transfers, then begin dispersing the assets to other accounts.

Aziz accepted his assignment with vigor and assured his masters that he would complete the task without fail. He realized, shortly afterwards, that none of the normal tools he had at his disposal for smuggling across the Strait of Gibraltar would work for such a large shipment needing delivery across the Atlantic Ocean, and with little more than a week to accomplish the task.

He was beginning to panic.

18

An unexpected guest arrived at the front gate to Aziz's home in Ville Nouvelle. A tall, alluring woman, wrapped in silk, her face hidden from the view of the guard by a celeste blue niqab, except for her stunning, almond shaped eyes. Eyes that miraculously shifted in color from sea green, to the cast of storm-cloud gray, as she subtly moved her head from one side to another. The guard looked directly into those eyes, and she overpowered him.

"I must speak with Aziz Harrak," she said.

The guard slowly regained his senses, "The master of this house sees no unscheduled visitors. You must go away now."

"He will see me, I assure you. Tell him that Avigail has come. I request sanctuary in his home, and I have news of the murder of Farouk Kateb."

The mention of Farouk's name caused the guard

to imperceptibly flinch. Farouk had been here many times in the past years, and his demise had caused the entire compound to go on high alert for nearly a month. The guard radioed back into the house for instructions. After a brief conversation with someone in the house, he opened the iron gates and escorted Avigail to a blue tiled bench in the gardens.

"I must keep you here until someone comes for you," he said.

"I have been here before, I need no escort," Avigail said.

"Forgive me, but until someone who knows you can positively identify you, you must remain here. If you are not who you say you are ...,' his voice trailed off.

A moment later, a heavy-set older woman in a long black burka emerged from the house and came through the gardens to where they waited. Avigail recognized her by her form and the way she moved. It was the head of Aziz's house staff, a woman who had been very unpleasant with Avigail in the past, when she accompanied Farouk Kateb to the house. Her mind raced for an instant, *What if she denies knowing me? They'll kill me before Aziz can see me.*

The old woman came within a safe distance and waved her hand for Avigail to remove the niqab that covered her face. She reached behind and unclasped the veil and let it fall to her shoulder. The old woman stared, then took a step closer, twisting her mouth and squinting her eyes with a look of uncertainty.

Avigail regained her confidence and stood up, which made her tower over the old woman. She looked down on her with those piercing gray eyes, "Don't pretend you don't know me, Amira. I have news of Ambassador Kateb's death to delivery to Aziz. He will want to hear this from me."

The older woman, Amira, lost her nerve. She turned to the guard, "Yes, this is Avigail, the consort of His Excellency, Farouk Kateb."

Avigail ignored the slight insult the old woman threw into her concession and followed her back into the main house. She had been here before, but still marveled at the beauty of the young man's home.

As they passed through the arched doorway, it was much like passing from one lush garden outdoors to another inside. An impossibly tall ceiling with skylights in the foyer and palm trees in sunken planters that reached thirty feet high, and they encircled an octagonal water fountain that gurgled a melodious tone which echoed off the surrounding walls of hand-painted tile. Beyond the fountain was a lounge that held several low tables with silk cushions and elegant carpets. A very typical interpretation of old Islamic culture, including a tall golden hash pipe in the center.

The two men in suits, one on each side of the foyer, with automatic weapons tucked neatly beneath their arms, reminded Avigail of the business that Aziz was in. Despite his architectural taste, he was a criminal, and this was a place of grave danger.

"Wait here until the master has summoned you," Amira said to her, pointing to a bench by the fountain.

Avigail reattached the veil on her niqab to maintain a respectful modesty in front of the house guards, even though Moroccan women were not bound by the same ridged customs as those who lived in more traditional Islamic countries. She waited patiently for twenty minutes before hearing the light footsteps of Aziz coming down the staircase.

He walked past her, seemingly without notice, and went into the lounge where he made himself comfortable on a cushion and motioned for Amira to bring him something to eat. She returned with a silver tray loaded with dates, olives, and a selection of cheeses, along with a gold-trimmed pot of black tea. She set it down on the walnut table without making the slightest sound, then poured a cup of tea for Aziz before leaving the room.

Aziz sampled a few olives, took a long sip of tea, then motioned to one of the guards to bring the woman to him. Since the death of Farouk Kateb, Aziz had assumed a new level of power in the Moroccan territories, and a higher standing in the criminal enterprises that were funding the great jihad. He was enjoying his status with heightened arrogance.

Avigail approached, being mindful that the young peacock required a delicate touch and a level of respect. If, at any moment, he found her to be insulting or disingenuous, he could have her dragged into the garden and murdered. No one would ever question his authority or decision. But Avigail had been trained from childhood, to manipulate and control men just like Aziz. He had no idea how outmatched he really was.

"As-salaam alaykum (peace be upon you)," she said as she entered the lounge.

Aziz looked up at her, and he was instantly struck by the eyes he remembered so well. Eyes that had first captured his heart when he was still a very young man and saw her for the first time in the company of Farouk, "Wa alaykum as-salaam," he answered after a moment's pause.

"Please sit and enjoy some food. I am eager to hear what you have to tell me about the Ambassador's assassination, and also, where you have been all these months. It was assumed that everyone aboard Farouk's yacht was murdered along with him. I was quite surprised to hear that you, alone, have miraculously come back from the dead."

She sensed his suspicion, and she gracefully lowered herself to a cushion on his right, being careful not to be too close, yet not too far away. She lowered her head and her shoulders beneath the silk cover in a very passive way. Then with a deep sigh, she began to tell her tale.

She recounted to Aziz the story of Farouk Kateb's intricate plan to bring together the three men who controlled the largest distribution network of heroin, hashish, and human trafficking in Africa, the Middle East, and Northern Europe. Men that he had been working in union with for several years. His plan was to murder them, seize control of their organizations, and unite them under the banners of Hezbollah and the Iranian backers. And murder these men, he did.

She also told him that an unexpected man had arrived in Monte Carlo, and tortured and killed Jean-Étienne Berger, the head of Banco Baudin, who managed all of the financial assets for Farouk's companies. Under direction of Farouk, Avigail had lured this man to Mallorca where he was killed by Farouk's assassin, Abd al-Rahman. She departed the port of Mallorca with Farouk, to his yacht, which was several miles offshore, and when they arrived, they were ambushed.

When she was sure she had Aziz's attention, she lowered herself further and whimpered at the distress of reliving the story. She reached up and lightly pulled at the niqab around her face as if it were suffocating her. Aziz took the bait.

"Please, remove this cover from your face. There is no need for it here," he said.

She nodded her head, then turned so that he

could reach the back and unclasp it for her. He pulled it free and her long black hair fell over his arms in shimmering waves of curls. When she turned back to face him, he was dumb struck by her beauty. In the few years since he had last seen her, he had forgotten how stunning a woman she was.

"Thank you, Aziz. You are so kind to me," she said.

She resumed her story and told him that in the initial moments of the attack on the yacht, she had thrown herself, in desperation, over the side and into the churning sea behind the boat. She had fully expected to drown, given that they were in the open sea and too far for her to swim to shore. The yacht had motored slowly away from her, and she witnessed the killers throwing Farouk's body over the side. Then in the distance the yacht exploded in a massive fireball and disappeared.

The explosion must have been seen from afar, because a short time later a fishing boat arrived and plucked her from the water, as she was nearly out of strength to continue. They took her back to Mallorca, where she hid from the police for many weeks, before stowing away on a vessel to Spain. For the last two months she had been traveling, and seeking help here and there, until she met an associate of Farouk. A Belgian named Gregor. He helped her with new clothing, a little money, and passage across the Strait of Gibraltar to Morocco.

She knew if she could make it to Marrakesh, she would be safe.

"And safe you are, my little dove." Aziz was deeply under her spell. "You may stay here in my home for as long as you like, and perhaps you can work with me as you once did with Farouk."

"You are very generous, thank you. I'm very happy to be back in a place, and with a man, who make me feel safe," she said.

19

Lucas answered the encrypted satellite telephone on his desk, "Hello, little sister."

"I love hearing that." Eliza said. "Listen, our company has just made a small purchase. You'll find it useful."

"What did Fairhope Group buy this time?"

"A very lightly used, two year old Gulfstream G550 Corporate Jet. Courtesy of the Sultan of Maladh."

"Does he know he sold it?"

"Yes, of course. He begged me to get rid of it for him. After two years, the leather interior doesn't smell new anymore, and he just can't bear it. So he buys a new one. I told him I had met a poor-country princess this year whose husband wanted to buy a used one, because they weren't wealthy enough to buy new."

"How much did we pay for this little gem?"

"The meager sum of fifteen million, a fraction of what a new one costs. I've also employed a pilot, a very loyal man who has worked with my travel and security teams for several years. I trust him implicitly. He will be arriving with the plane tomorrow at Palma International, at 12:30."

"You won't be coming with him? I was hoping to spend some time together before we leave for Curaçao."

"No. I'll be traveling by sea. You need to pick up Serge and fly ahead. I suspect you might need the time to do surveillance work before we arrive with the emissary. We should be there within the next seven to eight days, if the seas are kind. I will call you on the SAT phone when we are near."

"Ok, be safe. I'll be waiting for you."

20

MARRAKESH, MOROCCO

Aziz hadn't slept a wink during the night. He rose at 3:00 in the morning to pace about the house, then sat in the garden staring at the stars, and contemplating his options. This was his first big responsibility for his new patrons, and the pressure was breaking him.

He was given the chance to prove his worthiness as the rightful successor to his mentor, Farouk Kateb. He would take his place at the table and assume leadership of the distribution channels for the North African businesses that supported his brothers in Palestine and Lebanon. The businesses were disguised as commercial fishing operations and a few cargo vessels that delivered oranges and tangerines to ports in Spain, Portugal, and France. But the real products were hashish, opium, and tender young flesh.

Now, he was charged with personally insuring the

delivery of $1.2 billion dollars' worth of opium across the Atlantic Ocean to seal a new alliance, and verify the payments had been made into the established bank accounts, and the money was available for dispersion. Then return with a sample of young girls for the sheiks on the Gulf, who were the real financial backers of Islamic Jihad.

If all went well, he would be handsomely rewarded. He knew it. But with great responsibility comes great consequences for failure of any kind. It would likely mean his death. And the strain of that consequence was causing him to doubt every solution he came up with.

He knew nothing about deliveries made across great distances by airplane, because he had never even flown on one. All he knew was that airports are full of police and drug sniffing dogs, so that was out. He had only eleven days left, so his normal commercial shipping options would take too long to cross the vast ocean to Curaçao. What was he going to do?

THE TANGERINES HANGING on the trees in his garden began to glow like brilliant orbs on a Christmas tree, as the sun crested the sand dunes and struck them with first-light rays. He sat on the blue tiled bench near the fountain, slumped over with his face buried in his hands, and the sweat of fear soaking the back of his silk shirt.

Avigail came down the stairs and walked through the main salon of the house, and saw him sitting alone outside. The guards were nowhere to be found. She walked out to him. "Good morning, Aziz."

He looked up. His eyes were blood red, and flaps of skin hung from his young face like an old man's, "I can find no joy in this morning. I have a burden that I can find no solution for, and it will be the death of me."

"Is there anything I can do to ease your burden? Please let me help you," she said.

"You are only a woman, what could you do? This is a business matter, of great importance and urgent need."

She lowered her head as if to acknowledge his derision, and replied, "Yes, it's true, but His Excellency Kateb, trusted me with many important matters, and perhaps some experience I might have had while in his company would serve you. You have taken me into your home, and it would please me very much to be of service to you."

"Very well. I have been charged with delivering a very large order from our Iranian partners across the Atlantic Ocean to an island in the Caribbean, and it cannot go by airplane. I must accompany it personally, and no ship that I have access to is fast enough to make the voyage in less than eleven days."

Avigail walked slowly around the fountain, with her hands held together in front of her body. The sheer morning dress she wore, pulled snugly against her breasts and her slender waist, had Aziz's attention drawn to her for an instant, and away from his plight.

"I don't know if it would be an option you might think worthy, but as I arrived by boat yesterday in the port, I did notice that, anchored slightly offshore, was a magnificent yacht that I recognized very clearly as one belonging to an important client of His Excellency Kateb. I would assume he is now also an important client of yours, as you are rising to assume the leadership once occupied by His Excellency."

Aziz, shifted on the bench and straightened up, "How would the yacht of a client serve my needs?"

"I have traveled on these vessels many, many times, and His Excellency had one very much like this one. They can cross the oceans incredibly fast, perhaps in as few as six days, and it is a very luxurious way to travel. It would suit a man of your stature very well," she said. Then she added, "This particular yacht belongs to the Sultan of Maladh. He is the sole ruler of a small, but very powerful and wealthy country in the Gulf, and as I have overheard, a dedicated supporter of the Holy Jihad. Are you familiar with him?"

Not wanting to seem ignorant, Aziz lied, "Yes. I've never had the good fortune of meeting him, but I've been involved in several transactions that benefited the Sultan."

"I assumed you would have. In my work for His Excellency, I came to know the Chief Consort of the Sultan of Maladh, and she is regularly at home on this yacht, keeping it ready for his pleasure. The Sultan, like many men of his position, is often very generous with the loaning of his possessions to responsible men such as yourself.

If it would please you, I would be happy to contact the Chief Consort of the Sultan and inquire if it might be possible to have use of the yacht for a short period of time."

Aziz stood and rubbed his chin with his fingertips, "Yes. Yes, that might be an excellent solution. Make contact with her right away and advise me immediately."

"As you wish, my lord," she said. Her demure bow and smile made him feel powerful and confident again.

21

CÉRET, FRANCE

A cell phone sitting atop an oak dining table rang and vibrated across the surface at the same time. It kept ringing, until the little Frenchman nervously picked it up on the twelfth, "Oui?"

"Serge, where the hell were you?"

"Lucas! I didn't know it was you. I thought it might be the lawyers again."

"What lawyers? Are you in trouble again, Serge? I told you not to get into any more trouble, because we can't have people watching you if you are going to work with us."

"No! It's nothing. Just something about the taxes on my house. Don't worry. Do we have another job? Please tell me we have more work to do. I can't stand being in this crappy little cottage another minute!"

. . .

Serge Bonfiles lived in a dilapidated cottage that he inherited from his mother, in the mountainous outskirts of Céret, France. He was a native Frenchman who had joined the Foreign Legion the same time as Lucas. He was about the same age, and similarly, had virtually no friends or family. He had enlisted in hopes of finding a purpose for his life.

He was short and thin, with wiry ginger colored hair, wide ears and distinctively large teeth, which earned him the call-name, "Rat" in the squad. Lucas and Serge bonded almost instantly, being outcasts with a slight death wish. He had been by Lucas' side for nearly eight years in the Legion, and was known as the best armorer in the African theater, and a superior sniper.

He had a way with guns. He loved them, cared for them, and spoke to them secretly when no one was watching. And nothing he worked on ever failed to function in life-or-death combat.

He also had an unmanageable temper and went into fits of rage that frequently sent him to the stockade, and ultimately, out of the Legion. But when Lucas reemerged and needed help, the deadly serious kind of help, Serge was ready to stand by his side.

"Yes, Serge. We have a very big job. We are going to Curaçao. Can you be ready tomorrow evening?"

"Of course! What should I bring? Long range

shooting, close quarters? What about fragmentation grenades? I came across some for sale last month and put a few in stock."

"We won't know what we're going to need until we get there, so bring anything you want, but try to keep it to two large duffels. We'll have to keep it stored away in the jet until we clear customs inspections on the island. I'll be arriving at the private east runway at the airport in Montpellier about 9:00. Look for a G550, we're going first class across the ocean."

22

Diggs had both seats to himself in the Business Class side row, just in front of the main cabin exit. He had taken the Amtrak Acela Express from Washington D.C. to Grand Central Station in New York, and was now on the JetBlue flight from La Guardia, non-stop to Trinidad.

He reached into the small canvas briefcase sitting in the seat next to him, and pulled out a moleskin notebook and a pencil. He was still meticulously taking notes on the operation in Mallorca, even three months past.

He made notes in a peculiar shorthand about the speed of his entry, and the angle of his first shots. The impact effect and accuracy of the weapon. He made a note about Lucas, and his natural movements in the final moments of the combat. And one final note, (*add improvised weapons to Lucas' training regimen.*)

It was his nature to be thorough in recording every detail. Every new contact or person of interest, every potential future asset, everything that went as planned and everything that went wrong.

The recruitment of Lucas Martell had been successful, and now he understood why the woman funding the operation had insisted he find and recruit Lucas, before anything else. Lucas had proven himself under fire and was a motivated player. The future of the Fairhope Group was as much his destiny as that of its benefactor, his sister Eliza.

But the first targets for elimination, a money-laundering banker and an Algerian crime lord, had been relatively easy to identify and track. It would get more complex as they went from here. The men who might fall into their future "elimination list", would likely be more closely guarded and also harder to reach if they spent their time in hostile territory. Fairhope Group would need to expand its team of highly skilled operators.

Given that all of his old CIA false passports would likely be flagged at the international airport in Caracas, Diggs decided to fly into the airport of Port of Spain, on the island of Trinidad, just a stone's throw from the Venezuelan coastline. Trinidad didn't have the technology in place to connect with Interpol or the myriad of tracking tech used by wealthier South American nations and proxies.

It was ten o'clock at night when he landed. Dense low clouds, and a steamy late-summer rain beginning to fall. He leaned over to clear the low cabin door, and largely felt his way down the creaking rolling stairs attached to the airplane in the damp darkness. By the time he touched the tarmac it all came back to him.

He couldn't see the crumbling concrete buildings or shacks tied together with rusting corrugated tin among the tall palm trees, but he would have known he was in Trinidad all the same. That distinctive reek of week-old garbage, rotting fish and humid salty air. It hadn't changed since the last time he came through this little spy's corridor to the socialist capital of South America.

Trinidad was an island of extraordinary beauty, where the rich lived rich lives, and most of the populace survived in poverty and squalor. Like so many of the Caribbean islands, it had once been a busy slave-traders port, abandoned and left to fend for itself a hundred and fifty years ago.

He hailed a beat-up Toyota taxi, one of only two in service at this time of night, and they drove a short distance to the fishing village of Diego Martin, which lies on a point of land that reaches west.

Only twelve miles farther across the channel, another finger of Venezuelan jungle reaches back. It's a short crossing. A man who was really fit and a strong swimmer could swim that far in a few hours. But these waters, and all of the coastline that wraps around eastern South America, is treacherously famous for sharks. Just a short distance to the south lies the infamous French penal colony known as Devil's Island. Always within tempting sight of the mainland, but no one ever made the swim and lived to tell about it.

Diggs went straight to the fishing marina. He walked out along the soggy, slippery wooden pier in near total darkness, the only light on the path flickered through portals, and oil lamps perched on the decks of a few boats. Many of the fisherman were so poor that they lived aboard their craft.

Near the end of the pier, he found what he was looking for. A large open skiff with a tall bow and a decent outboard engine. A weathered old black man huddled beneath a plastic tarp on the deck.

The old man spoke Creole English, and while Diggs didn't understand everything he said through picket-fence teeth, the old man quite clearly knew what the tall Americano wanted. He negotiated a hard price. A ride across the channel in thrashing seas and total darkness wasn't something he was eager to do, but for five-hundred US dollars he would have killed his own mother.

They waited a few hours until the rain stopped and the wind died, then set off in the pre-dawn. It took forty-three minutes, rolling up and crashing down through the black water, before they saw the first lights flickering through the early morning ground-fog.

Just as the morning glow was coming over their backs, Diggs stepped off the skiff onto the mucky beach, just north of the Venezuelan village, Guiria. He bought a ticket on the only national bus line still in operation, scheduled to arrive in Caracas at 4:30 in the afternoon.

Along the journey, he had been practicing basic company fieldcraft, evolving into completely different characters at each stop. His clothing changed. His height changed with elevated or flattened shoes. His posture and gait changed. The hair on his head and his facial hair changed. And given that Facial Recognition software was now widely in use in the southern hemisphere, he used a very special variety of blending tape to pull and secure the loose flesh on his face in different angles, to throw off the connection points.

THE ONCE LUXURIOUS bus lines that transported passengers across Venezuela had fallen to ruin along with everything else in the country. The double-deck Mercedes was in need of a paint job and new tires. The rich black leather seats in the premier-class cabin were faded to the color of ash, cracked and torn and stained by all manner of things that people brought on board with them. Food and drink, small cooking stoves, goats and ducks and chickens; nothing was considered off limits now. Diggs seemed to be the only passenger without unusual cargo.

They passed through a few small towns on the full-day journey, but for the most part, he was lost in a view of endless palm trees blurring by, jungle covered hills, and the occasional glimpse of the sea to the right side. It was beautiful, and peaceful, as most of the Venezuelan countryside is and it ended suddenly in stark contrast to the vile urban sprawl of Caracas as they crested a low mountain.

The city consumed the landscape in all directions. Caracas was once a modern, beautiful place that rivaled places like Buenos Aires, Rio de Janeiro, and Miami. Carved from the jungles and hills of northern Venezuela, near the turquoise waters of the Caribbean Sea, it had exploded with cash during the early oil boom.

The president of Venezuela had been the secret instigator behind the formation of OPEC, and Caracas reveled in black gold. Then, the corruption brought the city to the ground. Now it was a crumbling wreck of violence, murder, and public humiliation.

Diggs could smell the change in the air, from fresh sea breeze, to the distinctive odors of a dilapidated city. He could also sense the changing mood of the other passengers on the bus. Their eyes flicked nervously out the windows, anticipating the dangers they would face the moment they stepped from the bus.

The predators were waiting, scattered about the loading platform and the street corners around the bus terminal. Watching for luggage, bags, and items that could be easily ripped from a person's grasp and run off with. They worked in teams. Bumpers and distractors, snatchers, and hand-off crews on motorcycles or bicycles.

Stepping off the bus was like stepping into a den of lions, but Diggs was carrying only an unappealing canvas bag, slung tightly over his shoulder and neck, and his height and physical appearance made him look like anything but an easy victim.

He walked out through the crowd, pushing forward with his shoulders, past the men who were hawking rides in their private cars, until he saw what he was looking for parked halfway down the block. The dark blue Chevrolet Malibu that Mathew Penn told him would be waiting.

He opened the passenger door and jumped in quickly, locking the door instantly. The young guy behind the wheel, maybe in his late twenties, with pale skin and brown hair cut close to the scalp, stood out amid the dark Latin crowds, and he looked frightened.

The kid shoved the car into first gear, fumbled the clutch, and it lurched and stalled. "Shit!" he muttered.

Then he pumped on the clutch and jerked the gear shift back and forth to find neutral. He reached for the key and twisted it half a turn, and the starter made a sound like metal files grating across each other.

"It's still in gear," Diggs said calmly.

"Sorry sir. I'm not used to a stick shift."

He pushed the clutch down again and pulled the stick back until it popped and wiggled freely in neutral, then turned the key again. The engine started, and he turned and looked at Diggs with a smile of relief on his face.

"If you sit here any longer, we'll have to fight our way out of this block," Diggs said.

"Sorry sir." Then the kid pulled away swiftly and headed toward the main Avenida Libertador.

"I want to go to Mariella Martinez' last known address in El Valle. Do you know where that is?" Diggs said.

"Yes, sir, but Station Chief Penn said I should bring you directly to the office at the embassy."

"Did Chief Penn tell you anything about me, and why I'm here?"

"He didn't say why you were here, sir, but I know who you are, sir. Or, who you used to be. Everyone knows who you were."

"Good. Take me to El Valle, and don't make me say it again."

23

Curaçao is one of a small chain of islands in the Caribbean that are nestled between the northern coast of Venezuela, and to the south of Cuba. Originally discovered and exploited by the Portuguese, it became part of the Dutch Antilles a few hundred years later. It started out as a central slave-trading port, conveniently located between South and North America, and easily reached from the coast of Africa by predictable trade winds that swept across the Atlantic in the warm months of summer.

When oil reserves were discovered in Venezuela in the early 1900s, the consortium of Shell and Exxon built a massive refinery on the island and controlled every facet of the business from pumping, refining, transporting, and marketing. Then in the early 1970s when world-wide oil reserves swelled and prices collapsed, the refinery went nearly bankrupt. Curaçao gained its independence from the Netherlands, and the refining operations were leased by the new local ownership to the Venezuelan company, PDVSA.

Given the island's origins in slave-trading, one of the oldest big-money enterprises in human history, it also has the distinction of being one of the earliest banking and financial centers in the modern world.

The oldest private bank in the western hemisphere still serves clients in the capital of Willemstad. And despite the fact that it signed on to the Foreign Account Tax Compliance Act with the United States in 2014, Curaçao remains a very darkly guarded tax haven for elicit investors around the globe.

Prostitution is a legal, regulated, and heavily taxed industry in Curacao, but oddly enough, only foreign women are granted temporary work permits. They are often gathered in an open-air marketplace known to the locals as, "Le Mirage".

Bram Bay, on the south side of the island, was originally built by the Royal Dutch Petroleum Company to serve as a docking and transshipment point for crude oil and petroleum products. Not long after the formation of OPEC, the Venezuelan oil giant, PDVSA, took a long term lease on the bay and all of its structures. And while it is a primary transfer point for Venezuelan oil, it has over the years become a hub of distribution for many other things.

In addition to the behemoth tankers that dock and fill their holds with crude to sail to faraway places, Bram Bay also serves the logistical needs of drug-traffickers and human-traffickers alike.

Rather fitting it seems, that this place prospers now in much the same way and serving the same vile businesses as it did when Curaçao was founded hundreds of years ago.

Bram Bay, Curaçao

Camila was shrouded in darkness and silence. She could only hear the raspy echo of air vibrating against the back of her throat as she breathed. Her ears had been stuffed with cotton balls, and an oily rag wrapped tightly around her eyes and tied behind her head.

Her eyes would have been useless anyway in the pitch black, but her ears would have heard the metallic resonance of the walls and the mechanical sounds from outside the shipping container that was now her personal prison.

Her hands were drawn to the small of her back, and zip-tied together with her ankles, which kept her in an excruciating backward arch. She was laying on a hard oak strip floor that smelled of chemicals and foul odors, but the discomfort was eased by the drugs.

After binding her and eliminating her senses of hearing and sight, her captors had forced a mixture of Methaqualone dissolved in a 120-proof Caribbean rum, down her throat with an automotive funnel. Within ten minutes, she fell into a near catatonic state.

When she was dragged from the van on the jungle road, Camila revealed her true nature. No longer a fourteen-year-old princess, she fought like she was possessed by a demon. Slashing with fingernails and teeth, and furiously kicking with sharp pointed leather sandals, she inflicted a few wounds on the two young men who first took hold of her.

Two larger men came to their rescue and seized her by the arms and legs to bind her, and she snarled and cursed them, "Let me go, you ugly mules!" Then she challenged them with her father, "Don't you know who I am? My father will cut your heads off!" But nothing she could do or say was going to change her destiny.

As the days passed, they allowed her to revive from the powerful depressant. Once a day, they freed her feet from the restraints so she could stand and relieve herself in a bucket in the corner of the container, and after the third day, she became willing to drink water as they placed a bottle to her lips, and eat the meager rations of food they offered her.

By the fourteenth day, she had ceased trying to

resist, call for help, or to speak when they came to attend to her. She was silent and submissive. But still, they kept her hands bound, and her eyes and ears covered. They were masters at the use of sensory deprivation in bringing an unwilling young girl to heel.

Very soon, she would be as gentle as a lamb, and would come to see the first person to remove her blindfold as her personal savior. She was not the first young girl, nor the hundredth, or even the thousandth, that these people had captured and conditioned. They were seasoned professionals in the world of slavery and human-trafficking.

As bad as Camila's situation was, she was still, in a sense, living a more privileged existence than others around her. She was isolated in her own small container and had an attendant who checked on her regularly. Her intake of water and food was being monitored, as well as her breathing and heart rate. She was a high-value capture, and they needed to insure her survival.

The other six girls who were taken from the van along with her were not so fortunate. Even though some of those girls had very wealthy parents, no ransom demands were sent. Their abductions were only window-dressing for the real target, Camila. To engage their parents in ransom negotiations could have exposed the operation, and the real prize was worth far more than meager insurance money.

All of the other girls were crammed into a small container together. Similarly bound and sensory deprived, but kept in a mild drug-induced drowsiness. They were offered water and a morsel once a day, and if they refused, they wouldn't get another chance until the next day. By the end of the first week in captivity, one of the girls had died from dehydration.

The timing, location, extraction of the victims, and disposal of evidence, had been nearly perfect. The kidnapping was executed with military planning and precision, and were it not for the miscalculation of the water depth at low-tide, the van and the remains of the driver and chaperone might never have been found.

24

EL VALLE, CARACAS

As they turned off Avenida Libertador onto a side road, the relatively clean highway asphalt changed to broken tarmac and gravel. The surface roads, in particular those leading into the destitute barrios and no-go zones, were never maintained or repaired. With each passing rainstorm, the old pavement receded a little more, and gave way to the rocky mud over which it was originally laid.

Office buildings, warehouses, and five-story apartment buildings that were newly constructed only a few decades ago, were rotting and collapsing. Once painted in vibrant Caribbean shades of blues, yellows, and red, they were faded and chipped and sprayed over with gang-tags and street-slang. Many of the original glass windows had been broken and replaced with plastic tarps stolen from construction sites and loaded trucks that paused a moment too long at an intersection.

With every block that passed, it had the feel of entering a war zone. The violent beginnings of the Bolivarian Revolution, it seemed, had never ended in El Valle. The concrete walls were a mottled mosaic of bullet holes and the scorched compositions of Molotov cocktails.

Both Diggs, and the kid driving the shiny Chevrolet, felt the cloak of being inconspicuous on the highway fall away from them here. They were visible and exposed now. Eyes were following them, trying to identify them, and gauging whether or not they represented a threat, or would make an easy target.

The police never came here, except in force, so they were obviously not cops. No one who lived here drove a vehicle like the Malibu, so they certainly weren't locals. The sheer recklessness of two men driving deep into El Valle in a nice car raised alarms up and down the valley. Young boys, armed with pipes, Louisville Sluggers, and the odd handgun, started gathering on stoops as they passed. Spotters on rooftops with cellphones were calling ahead.

"Your chief said he would send a gift for me, so I didn't have to worry about bringing my own. I think I might need it," Diggs said to the young driver.

"Yes, sir. It's in the glove box."

Diggs reached forward and pulled open the dash compartment, and pulled out a Glock 27, subcompact pistol. It had a full magazine loaded with .40 caliber S&W cartridges already in the grip, and two loaded spare mags. The pistol concealed neatly into his right front pocket, and he tucked the two mags into the left side of his waistband.

Every block deeper he drove into El Valle, the kid looked more nervous, and when Diggs armed up, a few beads of sweat broke out on his forehead.

Diggs noticed the kid's uncomfortable squirming in the driver's seat. "Sorry, I didn't catch your name, son," he said in a calm voice.

"Thomas, sir. Thomas Davies."

"Listen, Tom, you're gonna be just fine. Relax, do what I tell you to do, and we'll be out of here without a scratch. Ok?"

Tom looked over at Diggs, a CIA legend that he had been hearing about for most of the eighteen months he'd been employed with the agency. He was nervous just being in his presence and really didn't want to screw this up. But he was scared shitless right now, and he knew Diggs could smell it on him. Hell, everyone in the barrio could.

"Yes, sir. Just tell me what you need me to do," Tom said.

"Let's do a slow drive-by of the building first. Don't stop. You keep watching the street and buildings ahead, and I'll recon the apartment," Diggs said. "Here it is, next corner."

As they passed by the apartment building on the right, Diggs carefully scanned the ground floor entry, which was boarded over, and saw the rusty metal fire-escape ladder going up to the second and third floors from the side alley. The building looked completely abandoned, as did all of the others around it, and across the street.

"Go one more block, then do a series of right-hand turns to bring us back here. Then back the car into the side alley, and leave the front hanging out enough for you to watch the sidewalks both ways, while I go up the ladder to the apartment. The alley is completely bricked up from the back, so the only threat will come from the front or the sides. Once I'm up there, I can cover you from the window."

Tom looked the old agent in the eyes and tried to look tough. He pulled his Ray-Bans out of his shirt pocket, which was drenched in sweat from the August heat, and nodded his understanding. He drove around in a loop and ended up back in front of the dilapidated building, hit the brakes, smoothly dropped into reverse gear, and backed into the alley using only the side mirrors. He put it in neutral, left the engine idling, and pulled his own Sig Sauer pistol from his hip holster and laid it on the dash in plain sight.

Diggs smiled, "Nicely done. If you see anyone moving in the street, anyone, tap the horn twice."

He pulled the small Glock from his pocket and pointed it straight up the ladder, keeping his eye and the three-dot gunsights trained on the open window above him as he scaled the ladder to the third floor. As he reached the window and carefully scanned the interior, he could see the place had been ransacked. The other poor people in the barrio hadn't wasted any time cleaning out what little Mariella had owned, but the destruction was worse than you might expect from simple thievery. Someone else had been here.

The apartment was stone empty. Not a rug, a candle, a crate, or anything that might have some functional use left in it. There were pieces of trash and broken beer bottles in the corner, where someone had sheltered here for a short time. Maybe kids came to shoot smack and screw, but no one had moved in. The windows, if there had been any when Mariella lived here, had been pried out of the walls, frame and all.

Diggs went straight to the bathroom and stood there, looking at the toilet. The apartment hadn't had running water for a long time, and the toilet was cracked and stained the color of rust. He wondered if she might have remembered her training.

Nearly twenty years ago, Diggs had befriended, then recruited, young Mariella Martinez. She occupied a very special position in the Venezuelan oil giant, PDVSA, that gave her access to private meetings, files, and intimate knowledge of the comings and goings of important men. As part of her training, Diggs had taught her how to conceal small items in places where few people might look for them. The hollow underside of a toilet was one of those.

He used his foot to lightly push the rim of the foul ceramic throne, and it moved easily under the pressure. The bolts had been loosened. Then he gave it a solid kick and sent it tumbling over on its side, and it broke into four large pieces, scattering with a bang on the linoleum floor. From underneath, a dirty plastic bag fell out, twisted and wrapped tightly with duct tape.

He picked it up and went back into the main room and stood in front of the window where he had more light to see. Peeling the tape back, he could tell the package had not been sealed that long ago. The adhesive on the tape was still gooey and strong. He paused for an instant, considering that the thing he held in his hands had likely been in Mariella's delicate hands not long ago.

He pulled the tape off and untwisted the bag, then shook out the contents into his palm. The first was a piece of paper folded many times until it was small enough to fit into the concealed hiding bag. The second, a small photograph that was carefully rolled into a tube, like a cinnamon stick from a French cafe.

He slipped the folded paper into his pocket, then gently unrolled the photo.

It was a photograph of Mariella, sitting at a small bistro table in a restaurant. She was leaning forward on the table with her elbow, her hand tucked under her chin, and completely absorbed by the man who sat across from her. She was smiling, and happy, and had a look on her face that could only be interpreted as contentment.

Only a slight profile of the man across from her could be seen, as his back was mostly to the camera. But Diggs knew instantly that it was him. He couldn't quite remember the moment, but he recognized the restaurant. It had been a regular meeting place for the two of them. He wondered who might have taken the photo and given it to her. A friend perhaps? Or maybe it was a surveillance photo taken by one of his adversaries. It didn't really matter anymore.

He looked up and stared out across the smoke-filled valley, and the skyline of Caracas, trying to remember the last words he spoke to her before sending her back into the dangerous world of spies. He could picture the last meeting. He could see her face and smell the Chanel Coco Mademoiselle perfume that he'd given her only two days before the last time he saw her. But he couldn't remember his final words. Were they gentle and meaningful? Or were they merely last minute instructions?

He turned away from the window and glanced

around the pitifully filthy shell of a room. His heart clenched in his throat as he looked at what had become of her, of what life he had abandoned her to live.

A double-tap car horn snapped him back to the present.

25

Diggs turned back to the window and looked down, there was a small gang of young men, boys mostly, coming toward the parked Chevrolet. He went out the window and down the fire-escape in a flash and slipped past the car to meet them in the center of the street before they made it all the way across.

He glanced around at the young CIA driver, Tom, as he squeezed between the car and the wall, and saw him reaching for the pistol on the dash. He moved his head vaguely from side to side and silently mouthed the words, "*Be calm.*"

The leader of the gang was tall, and rail-thin from hunger. Maybe twenty five, and wearing a dirty rag tee-shirt and cut-off jeans. As Diggs came into the street in their direction, the other boys fanned out to either side of their boss. Diggs ignored them, making eye contact only with the tall young man in the middle, holding his gaze as he moved deliberately toward him.

Diggs moved with the same stoic, emotionless manner that he did in every potentially lethal situation he faced. It was his survival mechanism, absolute control. Nothing rattled him, nothing distracted him. In his peripheral vision he could see the others shuffling their feet and reaching for hidden objects, weapons, but once he had the leader's eye, he never set him free.

The leader was standing straight, his chin up, and shoulders squared to the front. He stayed cool as Diggs walked deliberately at him, all the way up until it looked like Diggs was going to plow through him. That was when his nerve broke.

He took a stumbling half-step back, then caught himself, just as Diggs arrived in his face. His gaze was transfixed by the old agent's stare, so he never saw the pistol coming up from the pocket. Diggs grabbed the front waistband of the thin man's pants with his free hand and pulled him in tight and jammed the muzzle of the pistol into his left eye socket, forcing his head back. The gang leader's back arched, his knees buckled, and all but two if his young comrades turned and scattered like cockroaches into the nearest crack or crevice of El Valle.

. . .

In precise Spanish, Diggs said, "I'm going to ask a couple of questions. If I think you are telling me the truth, I will let you live. If you lie, you die."

The two boys who hadn't fled the instant the gun came out, were ten feet behind. One was waving a rusty kitchen knife out in front and had a menacing scowl on his face like a cornered street dog. He was scared, but loyal to his leader. He was the most dangerous of the two.

The other had a triangular section of roofing tin that was ground to a gnarly point, and had duct tape wrapping for a handle. It looked more like a sorry prison weapon, and his face was wrenching with fear and doubt, his eyes flicked nervously back and forth between his partner and the pistol in Diggs' hand.

They were both determined not to abandon their leader but were terrified to come close enough to use their weapons. When they heard the Chevy's door pop open and saw Tom exiting with a pistol, they wheeled around and vanished into an alley.

"It's just you and me now," Diggs said to the street boss. He relaxed the pressure on the pistol just enough to let him bring his head upright and look at Diggs with his unoccupied eye.

"First question: did you know the woman who used to live here?"

"Si, Señor. Her name was Mariella," he said without hesitation.

"Who wanted her dead?"

"I don't know, Señor."

Diggs put more pressure on the gun and drove it deeper into his eye socket, "I told you, if you lie, you die."

"I swear on the holy mother, Señor, I don't know who wanted to kill her. But *El Mono* was here watching her for weeks before. Then he came to the apartment after the bombing."

"*El Mono*? The Monkey? Who is he?"

"He is a 'Sapeo' (a snitch)! He works for the old patrón of El Valle, the one they used to call The Butcher . The last time we saw *El Mono* here was the day after the Cubans bombed the *perrera*, but he is somewhere in El Valle almost all the time."

"Cubans bombed the truck full of people at the Palacio de Justicia? How do you know that?"

"Everyone knows, Señor! Whenever the common people are attacked with bombs, or tortured in *El Helicoide*, it's always the Cubans."

EVEN BACK IN the days of Hugo Chavez, the CIA had known that their real adversary in Venezuela was not the Venezuelans, but the Cuban DI operatives. They had been secretly orchestrating the direction of the government and its policies since the days of Che Guevara.

The president's personal bodyguards are Cubans. The men who approve every identification card, driver's license, voter registration, and applications for government aid, are all Cubans. They are the not-so-hidden directors of the grand play.

It's widely believed that the Cuban DI has stored in Havana a detailed list with personal information of every single living Venezuelan. When one steps out of line or becomes a potential threat, they know precisely how to find them and how to leverage their cooperation.

DIGGS RELAXED his pressure on the pistol, "Tell me about The Butcher. Who is he?"

"I have only heard of him. I've never seen him, but he used to be the most powerful patrón in El Valle. He controlled almost all of the drugs and women in Caracas for many years. People say that he was an important man in the government. But after Maduro took over as Presidente, people say The Butcher is not so powerful anymore."

Diggs let go of the man and slowly lowered his pistol. Then he reached into his pocket and pulled out a crisp one-hundred dollar bill. "I appreciate your honesty," he said, as he slipped it into the man's palm between them, where the exchange couldn't be seen.

The man looked down with astonishment at the bill in his hand. It was more than he could earn in five months working a regular job here, even if he could find one. Any humiliation he might have experienced in front of his crew at the hands of the foreigner was instantly forgotten.

"If you can find out who The Butcher is, I'll pay the same amount for that information too, but I don't have much time. Do you have a cell phone?"

"Si, Señor!"

"Here's a number for to you call and leave a message. Just leave The Butcher's real name if you find out. Nothing else. Understand? And the faster you find out, the better."

"Si!"

DIGGS HADN'T HEARD that name in many years, The Butcher. When he was stationed here during the Hugo Chavez years, there were constant rumors of someone in the government who was also the head of a major drug cartel and smuggling operation, but they never identified him.

"What happened to *be calm*" Tom asked, as Diggs came back to the car.

"Didn't I look calm to you?"

26

Tom took a deep breath of relief as they passed through the final block of El Valle and turned onto the main highway leading to Caracas. Only a few miles further, and the disparity between where the common Venezuelans lived and the central city where the wealthy and the government officials lived, was glaringly obvious.

Central Caracas was being carefully maintained to present an image of modernity and wealth; a place where civilized people of power lived. It was the final facade of a crumbling socialist empire.

Diggs could see the US Embassy building in the distance, a gaudy terra-cotta colored building that stood out against the high-rises and distant green mountains. Tom drove up to the side gate and parked on the street, and they came in through the Marine-guarded diplomatic entry.

Nothing in the Embassy had changed in the years since Diggs left, even the cheap brown carpets in the lobby were the same. Tom led him down the stairwell to the "cave", the deep labyrinth complex that existed below the visible building. It was a place that Diggs was intimately familiar with, having spent six years of his life running the CIA's Latin American Covert Operations from the belly of this building.

Mathew Penn was waiting for him. He extended his hand as he approached, "Bill, it's been a long time. Sorry to bring you back here for something like this. Let's go to the war room."

They walked down a long hallway, yellowish fluorescent lights flickering above, and worn, dry linoleum flooring that cracked and popped beneath their feet. They entered a room at the end of the hall. Inside, it looked more like a science lab. Beakers and bottles, test tubes, gas lighters on steel tables, and the walls were papered with charts and chemical formulas on one side, photographs on the other.

Hovering in front of the wall of photos was a young woman, standing with one arm wrapped around her midsection and her free hand folded beneath her chin. She had long ginger-colored hair that was carelessly twisted into a coil, boyish hips and skinny legs, wearing Levi's and Tony Lama boots, and an unflattering grey tee-shirt. She was rocking gently back and forth, in deep study, like a musical savant composing a symphony in her head.

Bill walked up and gazed over her shoulder, studying the photos as well.

"Do you see him?" the young woman asked without taking her eyes off the wall.

There were at least three hundred photographs pinned against each other. Random street photos, buses, photos of private gardens and public housing projects, it all looked like a chaotic collage.

"See who?" Bill asked.

Mathew Penn walked up beside them. "Bill, let me introduce you to our newest analyst, Beth Michaelson. We stole her away from a dead-end career at MIT. Beth sees things that no one else sees. Makes connections that no one else understands. She's the one who just figured it out."

Bill leaned in and looked Beth directly in the eyes to draw her attention, "Show me."

"My job is to connect the dots, but almost never are all the dots at one scene. So, when this investigation went active, I had them bring in evidence from any other events that seemed out of the ordinary over the past few weeks, from all over Venezuela. We keep the judicial buildings and all of the federal offices under surveillance, so I had good video records of that scene before and after the bomb. Then we pulled in evidence from a few others. An assassination attempt on a military officer, an explosion in a poor barrio, and then a weird one, a kidnapping case."

Bill asked, "What was weird about a kidnapping case? That's a way of life down here."

"It didn't match anything we had seen before. Seven teen girls, all from influential or upper-class families, snatched in the middle of trip to France. The chaperone and driver were murdered, and no ransom demands have been made. The girls just disappeared. And the father, who was paying for the whole thing, is a former Colonel in the Army, and if rumors are true, he was the leader of the Cartel of the Suns."

"With a kidnapping in that league, you might not even know about a ransom demand. The father has probably hired a private recovery team to negotiate the return of his daughter," Bill said.

"We've had him, his bank accounts, his phones, and everyone around him under watch. He's got a huge kidnap insurance policy in effect, and they haven't even assigned an investigator. He's not making any moves.

Luckily, the private school where the girls were picked up had security cameras in the front courtyard. That's where I found a clear photo of the driver, who hasn't been seen since the day of the kidnapping," she said, as she reached up and pointed to a photo of a dark-tanned Latin male, loading bags into the back of a blue van. "But this isn't the same driver who was found in the van when it came out of the sea."

"Do you know who he is?" Bill asked.

Mathew spoke up, "We don't know his name yet, but we know who he works for. And we know he was also connected to the truck bomb."

Beth slid her finger across the photos, and stopped on another grainy, black-and-white surveillance picture, and standing on the sidewalk in front of the Judicial building, looking down at his watch, was the same man. The regular *perrara* pickup truck was also visible in the photo.

"This 'Rico Suave' son-of-a-bitch shows up in a lot of places. After we got our hands on copies of other evidence collected from the scene, the only I.D. that had any interesting background at all was the woman, Mariella Martinez. I believe you knew her?"

"Yes, I knew her."

"I hope she wasn't a friend. Anyway, research showed she was gathered up with the execs from PDVSA back in 02. Her boss, it turns out, was feeding intel to the Cubans. And when I checked current video from the Cuban Embassy, look who shows up," she said, pointing to another photo of the same dark-tanned man.

"This wasn't an amateur-hour bombing with fertilizer and diesel fuel, Bill. The backpack bomb was constructed with Semtex. We found residue over the entire block, so it wasn't difficult to get samples, and we've been doing the chemical analysis to get an origin signature," Mathew said.

"And? Where's it from?"

"Czech Republic. A very old batch, probably when it was still Czechoslovakia and under the thumb of the Russians."

"That makes it seem even less likely to me that Mariella was the primary target. Why would they waste something like Semtex to assassinate a protest organizer? It's a little overkill, wouldn't you think?"

"Unless there's something much bigger going on here, and they thought she posed a serious risk."

27

MOROCCO

Aziz tried to appear calm with Avigail sitting next to him, but he periodically turned and glanced at the truck that followed closely behind the Mercedes sedan. Ahead of his car, was another with four heavily armed men, and at the tail of their caravan was yet another car bristling with men and weaponry, guarding the rear. The six-wheeled transport truck in the middle was carrying the cargo, two shrink-wrapped pallets of boxes labelled as "Canned Tangerines", but which in truth contained pure opium.

The drive through the scrub desert and rolling dunes between Marrakech and the port town of Essaouira was the longest three hours of Aziz's life, because his life depended entirely on the safe delivery of those pallets. Getting them loaded aboard the private yacht that waited in the harbor was just the first step in a long journey.

As they drew closer to the ocean, the wind intensified and the fine sand of the Moroccan coast swirled across the road in front of them, obscuring the view at times so that Aziz couldn't even see the lead car. Avigail could see his hands turning pale as he subconsciously clenched his fists, she laid her hand on the black leather seat and allowed it to slide just close enough to touch the edge of his. It was a bold gesture, but it served its purpose by distracting him.

"There it is," she said, as they rounded a high dune and suddenly looked out over Essaouira and the harbor. The water within the jetties was a dark emerald green, like Avigail's eyes, but beyond, the oceanic current turned to gray. Just outside the harbor, the massive yacht was anchored and waiting patiently for its TransAtlantic cargo.

Aziz looked up and was astonished at the size of it. He had been aboard Farouk Kateb's yacht a few times, and thought it must surely have been the largest in the world, but it was minuscule compared to the boat that lay waiting beyond the reef, just for him.

Built by Blohm & Voss in the Netherlands, the yacht was three hundred feet long with four decks and a helipad. Painted pearl white with gold trim around the decks and the captain's observation platform, it had a deep long chine in the bow for breaking ocean sized waves, and full radar navigation equipment mounted above the bridge. She was built to navigate the oceans of the world at will, with speed and luxury.

Only a few shipbuilders in the world create private mega-yachts of this size and caliber, and only a handful of people in the world can afford them, the mega-rich of the rich.

"The Sultan of Maladh must be a very important man," Aziz muttered.

Avigail responded, "His Chief Consort has told me that the Sultan is from a line of rulers in Maladh who have history back almost as far as the stories in the Koran. His ancestors have ruled the island nation for all of recorded time. It will be my great pleasure to introduce you to the Sultana very soon. She will be joining us for the voyage across the ocean."

"She is going to join us? For the entire trip?" Aziz appeared disappointed, as if he thought he might have the comfort of the yacht and crew, and the private company of Avigail, all to himself for the next week.

"Yes. We were very fortunate that she was still here with the Sultan's yacht, because they were only stopping in Essaouira briefly for fuel and provisions to cross the ocean. The Sultan has entrusted her to oversee the transfer of his yacht to his private island, near the British Virgin Islands. He wanted it there to accommodate his many important business associates for a private party."

"Yes, it was very fortunate," Aziz said.

"Fortune favors bold men," Avigail answered. She smiled, and felt his uneasiness melting further away as she gently stroked his ego.

THE FORTY FOOT LONG, open bow motor launch powered out to the yacht with the two pallets safely wrapped and tied. As the boat approached, several crew members stood waiting alongside to tie up and activate a small crane and winch that was normally used to hoist the yacht's smaller landing craft. They used the crane to pull up the pallets and place them down below the decks in a water-tight storage area.

Aziz and four of his armed guards stood on deck and carefully watched every move. There was only one tense moment in the transfer, but it had nothing to do with the handling of the cargo.

As they were raising the second pallet from the motor launch, a tall woman, covered head to toe in saffron colored silk, with only her eyes and the creamy skin of her cheeks visible, stepped out onto the lower deck. She was flanked on each side by two men in tailored suits. Aziz's men, who were not well trained and very nervous about their assignment, turned and drew their pistols.

The two men in suits immediately drew H&K MP5 submachine guns from beneath their coats and stepped forward in front of the woman, aiming their weapons at Aziz and his men. The woman walked calmly toward Aziz, and her guards came along slightly ahead of her, as if they could sense her every move, and where she went, they moved as if a part of her.

"If you continue to point your weapons at me, my men will kill you and throw your bodies to the sharks," she said without the slightest hint of fear.

Aziz was startled. First by having automatic weapons pointed at his face, and secondly from being chastised by a woman. "Lower your guns, fools!" he said to his men. Then he turned back to the woman in saffron silk, "Who are you?" he said, before Avigail could intervene.

One of the guards, Mohammed, stepped forward another step and drew his gun barrel directly in line with Aziz's nose, "You are addressing the Sultana of Maladh, Chief Consort to His Highness, the Sultan! And you will show respect for her, or I will end your life."

Aziz took a step back and his knee faltered for an instant.

The tall woman spoke again, "Understand, you have been welcomed aboard a vessel that belongs to the Sultan of Maladh, and we will treat you as we would any guest who enters his lands. This yacht is as much a part of the Sultan's kingdom as his palace in Maladh. But if you violate the laws of the Sultan's kingdom while you are here, you will be punished just as swiftly, and it is my duty as the Sultan's Chief Consort to see it done."

Aziz had never encountered such a woman. She had a powerful demeanor and a strength that shone in those piercing green eyes. He had never felt fear in the presence a of woman before, but this one was different.

He acquiesced to her demands, "I offer my most humble apologies to the Sultan of Maladh and to his Chief Consort. We are most grateful for the hospitality being granted for this voyage."

Her posture softened and she lightly tilted her head forward, "We are honored to have you and your companion Avigail, as our guests. But we do not have accommodations available for your guards. I can assure you, as guests of the Sultan, you will be guarded quite well to your destination."

Aziz turned to Avigail and spoke in a low voice, "You didn't tell me this! I cannot travel with the cargo and no one to guard it!"

Avigail responded, "I was not aware of these conditions, please forgive me. But, it seems to me that there was no other opportunity to fulfill your obligation to deliver these items to Curaçao in such a short time. I trust the Sultan of Maladh and his people to keep us safe, and by coming with you, my life is in the balance as well."

He sighed and gritted his teeth, then forced a

smile on his face and turned to the Sultana, "Again, we are grateful for the Sultan's generosity."

THE TWENTY-PERSON CREW of the Sultan's yacht, aptly christened, "Abaasa", was regularly replaced with new members from many different countries. The cooks, maids, mechanics, and deck hands rotated often. Only the Captain of the vessel, two navigation officers, and one marine maintenance engineer, were retained permanently. So it was completely normal that a new service crew was taken aboard Abaasa in Gibraltar, before sailing through the Straight and around the shore of Morocco to the port of Essaouira.

What no one was aware of, other than Eliza and Avigail, was that the entire crew was composed of hand-picked members of the Israeli Mossad and a few private citizens who often volunteered to work for them. The yacht was harboring one of the most elite kill teams in the world.

28

ABOARD THE YACHT, ABAASA, IN THE ATLANTIC OCEAN

Eliza bolted upright in her bed from a terrible dream. A dream of violent men, grabbing, twisting arms and legs, and beatings. She could clearly see the face of Farouk Kateb, the man who sold her as a child to the Sultan of Maladh.

She had taken her revenge. Killed him months ago; looked into his eyes as he was rolled in a lush Persian carpet, then vanished beneath the waves in the Mediterranean. Then she watched from a great distance as his yacht was rendered to splinters in a fireball.

And yet, he still came to her some nights, to torment her further. This dream had other elements that disturbed her, too. An underlying feeling that Farouk and his henchmen had been taken just a little too easy. As if things had fallen into place with support from a hidden source, and not just fate.

She threw the covers off and stepped out of bed, pulled a large wool shawl around herself, and walked to the port-side window of her estate cabin. The sun was rising to their back, the waves reflecting the orange cast, and the western horizon in front was shifting from gray to blue over a calm ocean.

The news that came from Eli Moskarov had unsettled her. That someone had picked up the helm of Banco Baudin's clients immediately, and was carrying forth with the businesses of terror, corruption, and human trafficking.

Could this person, whoever they were, have been involved somehow in the Mallorca killings? Had the Fairhope Group been used to kill evil men, only to open the path for another to assume power?

Could they be walking into another deadly mission, at the behest of an unseen director?

29

BRAM BAY, CURAÇAO

Camila was succumbing to her pitiful existence of total isolation and sensory deprivation, hovering at the threshold of hopelessness, and begging God for a merciful end.

Then it happened.

Still blinded, deafened and tightly bound, she recognized the intimately familiar vibrations coming through the wooden floor of the container. The lock being twisted and dislodged, the heavy steel bolt grinding sideways and the vacuum of air in the metal prison "popping" as the large door unsealed and swung open.

The dank moist air rushed over her bare arms and legs, then she could feel the fresh salty breeze circulating in.

In the first days, her long hair would flutter as the air moved in and out, but now it lay matted and soiled, and sticking to her face and the greasy floor. It was once the color of dark mahogany wood and shined in the sun. She kept it in a long ponytail and pulled to the front across her left shoulder, which highlighted her best profile.

But now her hair was blackened and dull with weeks of sweat and oil and foul hands. She couldn't see it, but she could smell it, and in a single moment of vanity during the second week of her ordeal, she considered that she would have to shave it completely off when this was over. But as the weeks passed, the hope of this ever being over had drifted away.

She relaxed and prepared herself as she felt the light padding of footsteps coming closer. It was the same every day. A large hand would grip her firmly around her thin upper arm and pull her upright onto her knees. The clasps on her ankles would be freed, and she could feel the chain that connected them thump on the floor. The firm grip would then lift her to her feet and hold her sympathetically for a moment, until the blood flowing into her legs allowed her to stand on her own.

She would be guided a short distance to a corner, where a bucket waited for her. Whoever guided her, assisted with her clothing so she could relieve herself, then returned her to the original spot on the floor. The oak planks were always still warm as she lay back down.

On this day, the person who attended to Camila

noticed that as she was lifted to her feet, she made the very slightest gesture. Not quite a smile, but an indebted expression that let them know she was grateful for their attention. It was exactly what he had been waiting for.

After returning Camila to her spot on the floor and reconnecting the locks around her ankles, the man did something that startled and amazed her. Her held her face in his hands for an instant.

They were coarse and hot, but he held her cheeks softly and lightly swept away a strand of wet hair with his thumb. After what seemed a lifetime of isolation, his touch was like that of an angel, and tears suddenly swelled in her eyes.

Then the coarse hands went one step further. They slid gently to the sides of her head and pricked lightly at the wax-soaked balls of cotton that were driven deeply into her ear canals. Neatly trimmed fingernails pried the cotton loose and pulled them free.

The sensation was the same as the sealed door to the container opening with a pop and the fresh air rushing in to fill the vacuum. Her ear drums were ringing and thrumming with vibrations, and her brain was quickly trying to make sense of real sound waves. The expanse of her world had just been doubled, and she felt the rush of adrenaline flowing through her body.

"Don't cry my love, I'll take care of you," the voice said.

She couldn't speak. She had been silent now for a long time, but a faint gasp and whimper escaped her mouth as she heard his comforting words. His voice was strong but caring. She hung on the sound of it as it echoed against the steel walls, then the tears started flowing freely through the blindfold and down her face.

"You've been such a lovely girl, Camila. I won't let them put these back in your ears anymore," he said. "And if you keep behaving well, I'll be able to free your hands and feet, and let you see again very soon. Would you like that?"

Camila nodded and smiled.

"Listen carefully and remember my voice. My name is Raphael, like the saint. You know of Saint Raphael, don't you?"

Again, she nodded her head and the tears flowed.

One of the coarse hands reached up and touched her face again, and she let her head fall into it for the pleasure of his caress.

RAPHAEL RELEASED her constraints with carefully measured steps, over the coming days. And when at last he freed her hands and pulled the blindfold away from her eyes, his face was the first thing that came into view.

As if emerging freshly from a dark womb, she squinted and blinked against the violent sunlight, then slowly, her vision returned. He was the most beautiful thing she could remember ever seeing in her life. The man who had saved her from desolation, misery, and her imagined certain death. The most important man in her world.

It was a technique used for hundreds of years on captives, enemy combatants, and anyone whose mind one wished to control. The human mind is a fragile thing. Easily set off balance and influenced by fear. And when completely deprived of the senses that paint the richness of life around us, the mind loses all concept of time. Minutes become hours, hours become weeks, weeks become years.

In Camila's mind, she had lived an eternity in the confines of the container. Abandoned by her father, who she thought surely would have come for her by now, and by all others who might rescue her. The only man who loved her enough to rescue her now was the handsome Cuban standing in front of her, the angel Raphael.

"I have a surprise for you, Camila," he said.

Her eyes widened and she smiled like a small child anticipating a gift. "I love surprises," she said.

"I'm going to take you to a beautiful home by the sea, and you can bathe and wash your hair, and I'll give you a pretty new dress. Then we'll eat a wonderful lunch of fresh fish in the garden. Would you like that?"

"Oh, yes!"

"Good. Now I've risked my own life to take you away from this place, so please be good, or the other men might hurt both of us. Ok?"

She stared adoringly into his eyes, "I'll do anything you say, Raphael."

He wrapped a large towel around her, then picked her up in his arms and carried her down the steps from the container and sat her in the passenger seat of a black Mercedes sedan.

The car reminded her of her father's, but she couldn't remember Esteban hardly at all. He was only a vague shadow in the back of her mind. Raphael got into the car, reached across and pulled the safety belt down over her and buckled it snugly. He smiled warmly at her, then glanced at his watch before starting the engine and turning onto the road that ran along the rocky shoreline.

Camila was mesmerized by the turquoise sea as they drove along. It rippled and sparkled like diamonds as the early morning sun glanced across the wave tops, and she could see huge, fat-bellied ships, on the far horizon. It didn't occur to her that the sun was now rising to face her with the Caribbean on her right side. All the times before when she had ridden in a car along the shore in the morning hours, the sun had risen at her back.

The thirty-minute ride passed easily. Raphael laughed as she rolled down the window and held her face out into the sun and wind. "We're here," Raphael said, as they pulled into a coral-shell driveway lined by tall palms on each side. The tires rolled along and the sound was like crunching eggshells, Camila's spine tingled and her ears rejoiced at the wonderful noise.

As they approached a scrolled iron gate, two guards dressed in green leaf camouflage uniforms stepped forward. One held his hand up to stop and moved to the left side of the Mercedes. He had a radio in his other hand and a pistol on his side. The other guard had a black automatic rifle slung across the front of his body, and a menacing scowl on his face. Camila stiffened and sat straight up, then frantically pawed at the button to raise the window.

"Don't be afraid, these men work for me. You're safe," Raphael said assuringly.

As the guards recognized him, they stood immediately at attention and saluted smartly, then quickly opened the gate.

The house was large and strangely shaped. It was nothing like anything Camila had ever seen in Venezuela. It was square and plain, like a two story gift box, with a shining metal roof. And as far as she could tell, its only interesting feature was the brilliant blue color it was painted. A glowing indigo, with a terrible contrast of tangerine window frames. Like something a child would paint in a book where the violent shock of color was the only point of it all. It was hideous, and at the same time, wonderful to eyes that had held nothing but blackness for the longest time.

The car stopped in front of the house, and two more armed guards wearing casual island clothing came out the door, followed by a plump woman with short gray hair wearing a housekeeper's uniform. Raphael stepped out and opened the door for Camila and extended his hand. She took hold with both of hers and pulled herself to her feet, then leaned lightly against the man who had rescued her.

"This is Diana. She keeps the house and cooks for us. She will show you to your room and draw a nice hot bath for you," Raphael said.

The housekeeper smiled and beckoned her to follow her into the house. Camila first looked up into Raphael's eyes for his approval. "Go on, it's alright. No one will hurt you here. I will meet you on the veranda for lunch in an hour." Then he released her trembling hands and gently pushed her forward.

She walked slowly through the front door, her eyes held down to avoid contact with the other two men. The woman was partway up the stairs as Camila paused at the bottom, unsure if she had the strength to climb the winding case to the second floor. Seeing her hesitation, she came back down, took her by the elbow and patiently steadied her as they climbed the stairs together.

"Your bath is waiting, and I've put out some fresh clothes for you, miss. Would you like me to help you undress or help to wash your hair?" the housekeeper asked.

"No, thank you. I'm strong enough to bath myself."

After the woman had left the room, Camila slid off her long school uniform skirt, then unbuttoned the white blouse that now looked like a grease rag in a workshop, letting it fall to the floor. Her panties stuck to her bottom as she pulled them off and stepped away from them. She looked down at the soiled clothes as though they couldn't be hers. She had never worn anything so disgusting. She kicked them across the floor, then turned and walked into the bathroom.

As she entered, she was immediately confronted with a large mirror, and froze in horror.

Over a month of being bound and confined in total darkness, malnourished, dehydrated, and laying in filth, had left her unrecognizable, even to herself. She stared at this grotesque wretch in the mirror before her.

Her skin was dull and dirty and smelled like rotting salt brine. The bones in her shoulders and ribcage bulged through the thin covering, and the plump young breasts that were just beginning to grow, had withered into lifeless folds of flesh.

Her mahogany hair looked like a discarded floor mop. Gray strands of twisted and matted string with a pungent oily stench. She stared at herself in disbelief. Her body began to shake in light spasms, and finally, she burst into tears.

She allowed herself only a short time to cry, then turned to the large ivory colored tub that was steaming with hot water. She steadied herself with a hand on the edge and reached one foot over the side and into the water. Then she stepped in with the other foot and eased herself down into the soothing water, pausing with a flinch as her bottom, raw from being unable to even clean herself, stung for just a moment. Then she settled deeply into the tub and slid back, submerging her face and head below the water.

As she reemerged, she could see the oils and dirt coming free from her and floating away. She smiled, "This can all be washed away," she said to herself. "Everything that's happened to me can be washed away."

30

Mathew Penn was twenty-six years old when he was first assigned to the CIA's office in Caracas. He was one of the rare direct-from-college recruits who had always dreamed of being a spook.

He excelled in almost every area of general spy-craft during his training at "The Farm". Then spent the next several years working out of the Miami office and learning the complexities of the various agency involvements across fifteen different Latin American countries and learning Spanish.

When he was assigned to work with the CIA legend, William Diggs, in the Caracas office, which was the nerve center of the National Clandestine Service, he knew he was on his way to fulfilling his dreams. Diggs had done it all, and his signature on a few great performance evaluations could make Mathew's career soar.

But, it never happened.

Diggs abruptly left the Caracas office for an assignment in the Middle East, not long after the failed Coup d'etat of Hugo Chavez, and Mathew arrived in Venezuela assigned to work under the guidance of a lesser qualified Station Chief. Diggs returned a few times for brief assignments, and Mathew at least got to work with him and developed a professional rapport. But it wasn't the launchpad he thought the assignment could have been for his future.

He languished in the agency-hell of obscurity for the next decade and a half, as the coups, civil wars, and communist threats in Central America all became less important than what was happening on the other side of the world in the Gulf. The United States was now at war with a new and far more vicious enemy, Islamic Extremism.

Now, Mathew had finally been promoted to Caracas Station Chief himself, but unless something miraculous happened that brought his talents to the attention of Langley, he would end up wasting away here.

In his mid-forties, with a gleaming bald pate and sagging middle, his dreams of being a super spy were long gone. The best he could hope for was to become a formidable bureaucrat back in Virginia and hobnob with politicians on the White House lawn. Maybe he'd give the occasional interview on CSPAN or get a few agency spokesman roles on the Washington pundit TV shows.

But perhaps fate had finally smiled on Mathew Penn. The winds of fortunes had shifted and brought the Muslim extremists across the Atlantic, and into his domain. If he could foil one of America's greatest current threats in the Middle East from securing an alliance with the Communists and Socialists in Central America, it would make him an instant star in the CIA.

If he played his cards right, he might also have a shot at nailing the most notorious Cuban DI assassin in the world today.

HE WALKED through the open office area where most of the Central America Desk analysts and support staff worked in cubicles with low walls around them, so everyone could always see what everyone else was doing, and so the CCTV cameras in the ceiling could clearly record their every move. Computer access and searches were monitored, and all landline telephone conversations were recorded, even the Station Chief's, so he always had to be conscious of what he was saying and who he accepted calls from.

The CIA trusts no one completely, including their own.

He went into his private office at the head of the

room. It had sound-proof glass walls with dark drop shades, and no cameras. He locked the door behind him as he entered, hit an electronic remote to lower the glass covering, sat down at his desk, and turned on his computer.

The telephone rang on his desk and he answered before the second ring.

"Chief Penn, a call just came in asking to speak to the Station Chief. He said his name is Esteban Aguera," his switchboard operator said.

"I'll take it."

He put the receiver back down, and the call immediately rang through. He waited until the third ring this time before answering, "Station Chief Mathew Penn. Who am I speaking to?"

"Señor Penn, this is Esteban Aguera. Given that I once held a senior rank in the military in the previous administration, I assume that your agency has a file on me."

"I'm afraid I know nothing about you Señor Aguera, but how can the CIA be of assistance to you?" He could hear Esteban take a deep measured breath and exhale.

"My daughter was kidnapped several weeks ago, along with six of her friends in Barcelona. You have heard of this, yes?"

"Yes, I remember hearing something about a series of kidnappings, but that's a matter for local law enforcement."

"The men who took my daughter were not local criminals, Señor Penn, and this has nothing to do with ransom. The men who did this are from another country that is a sworn enemy of America, and they want something from me that will have a very profound effect on your country."

Mathew waited to answer. "Go on, I'm listening."

"I want to discuss an arrangement with your government. I have information that could be very valuable in stopping a great threat to your people. But I will only speak to you and no one else beneath you. I need to be assured that I am talking to the highest ranking officer of the CIA there. Someone who can make decisions and commitments to me."

"You're speaking to the right person. Where would you like to meet?"

"At my hacienda on the coast. I'm sure you can find it."

"I'm not familiar with your residence, Señor, but I'll find the directions. I'm free tomorrow afternoon. Will that be convenient?"

"Yes. I will tell my guards to expect you and allow you through the gates."

31

Driving out of the poverty-stricken war zone that was now Caracas, Diggs welcomed the rolling hills and jungled landscapes that lay between the city and the sea. He had hated the jungles too, after spending time in Cambodia and Laos in the seventies. But just like here, there were always locals who stayed in his mind after he was gone. People who, in some way, reminded him that there was something good about every place he had ever served with the agency.

As he and Mathew drove out to the private estancia of Esteban Aguera, he wasn't sure that Esteban would be one of those. One of the people who inspired him. They were only five minutes away when his cellphone vibrated in his pocket. He pulled it out and saw the "Missed Call" message, which meant he likely had a voicemail waiting.

He dialed his message retrieval line, and there was a voice message from an unknown number. A young man with a thick barrio accent muttered, "The Butcher was Colonel Esteban Aguera," then quickly disconnected.

His lips pursed for an instant, but he tried to stay focused. He knew Mathew was probably watching his reacts to the call. He turned his head away and acted bored with the passing landscape, lightly tapping his finger on the armrest.

"Anything going on I need to know about?" Mathew asked.

"No, just a message from the electrician back home. Said it's going to cost a fortune to bring the old house up to code. I should just have it demolished and build a new one."

"Are you going back to Winchester when this is all over?"

"Maybe. But when is anything really over?" He turned to face Mathew and gave him a rare sarcastic smile.

In his head, the wheels were beginning to turn. An ex-Chavez crony and military henchman, who just had his daughter kidnapped by the Cuban Intelligence Directorate, calls the CIA to ask for a deal. If the neighborhood informant was to be trusted, Esteban Aguera was also a former cartel boss, once known infamously as, *The Butcher*. And, he may have had something to do with the murder of Diggs' asset and lover, Mariella Martinez.

Mathew broke his concentration, "We're almost there."

The GPS indicated to "turn left" on a narrow gravel road, and Mathew followed along the path deeper and deeper into a vine-covered jungle. It appeared to go nowhere, or at least, nowhere they really wanted to get caught in an ambush or a firefight. Diggs pulled his Glock from its holster, checked the round in the chamber, and slid it under his right thigh with his hand on the grip.

After a mile and a half, the dense canopy opened and they found the way blocked by a massive iron gate. As the car came to a stop, two men in full camouflage and carrying Russian Kalashnikovs stepped out behind the gate pillars with the rifles aimed at the car. Diggs started to pull the Glock out.

"Easy Bill. They're expecting us."

He slid the pistol back beneath his leg, and put his hands up on the dash where the guards could see them. Mathew showed both his hands, then slowly pulled a lanyard I.D. from under his shirt and let the guard inspect it when he came to the window. "Señor Aguera requested our visit," he said.

The guard looked closely at the photograph on the badge then at Mathew's face, then spoke into a handheld radio. The iron latch clanked as the gate swung open on squeaky rain-soaked hinges. They drove through and followed the drive another two hundred yards before coming to the main house. Diggs tucked the Glock into its holster on his hip and pulled his shirt tail over it.

Esteban lived in a Spanish colonial estancia built in the middle of a Venezuelan jungle. It had a circular driveway in front bordered by vibrant red hibiscus, a rich green lawn, and leveled pasture around the sides and the back that was big enough to land a private jet. "Pretty nice place for a simple public servant," Diggs said.

"I don't think there's anything simple about Aguera."

Two more guards materialized from nowhere, standing on each side of the car. "These men are professionals. Likely been part of Aguera's private army for a long time. My guess is there are fifty more in the jungle that we can't see," Diggs said.

Mathew turned his head nervously left and right. He didn't have the years of field experience that Diggs did, and the guns were starting to make him uncomfortable.

The guards waved them both out of the vehicle, then motioned for them to raise their arms and be searched for weapons. With his hands still outstretched, Diggs pointed down to the Glock on his hip, and the guard pulled it out of the holster and laid it on the roof of the car. Mathew followed his lead, and the other guard took his Sig Sauer from his hip.

"My men will take good care of those until you are ready to leave," Esteban said, from the front steps of the house.

As they walked up to the estancia, Diggs picked out five different security cameras in the trees and roof line. Two of them rotated as they walked forward. He also caught a bright glint of sunlight flashing from a cliff ledge, about four hundred meters above the estancia. He knew it was the large objective lens of a sniper scope reflecting the light directly at his head. Mathew seemed oblivious to everything accept Esteban waiting with an outstretched hand.

Diggs took note of Esteban's manner as they approached. He had his hand directed for Mathew to accept it, but his eyes never left Diggs. It was as if he already assumed Mathew was less significant and didn't warrant eye contact.

"Gentlemen, please follow me."

They walked through a salon with terra-cotta tiled floors and tall ceilings with dark wood beams. The furniture was large and luxurious but looked as though no one ever sat on it. The room had the appearance of being decorated for show, but it was sterile and uninviting.

He led them down a long hallway, with glass along the right side that looked out to the pasture behind the house and then into a private study. Two black leather chairs sat facing a large red mahogany desk. On the walls behind the desk were photographs of

Esteban, twenty years ago in military uniform. Candid photos of him and Hugo Chavez, military parades and medal presentation ceremonies. Even one with Esteban and Fidel Castro.

"Please have a seat," Esteban said.

DIGGS SAT stoic and straight in his chair. Mathew did the talking and he didn't seem at all interested in the surrounding photos, the history, nothing, as if it was either meaningless to him, or things he'd seen before.

Mathew went straight to the point, "What do you want from the CIA, Señor Aguera?"

Esteban sat silent for a moment. The South Americans always like to chit-chat before getting down to business, and the bluntness of Americans always felt uncivilized.

"I want out of Venezuela. I want out of the cartel, and I want out of this fucking life," he answered. "And I want my daughter with me."

"That won't be easy, Esteban. And it won't be cheap. What are you willing to do for it?"

Diggs kept his eyes on Esteban to watch his reactions and subtle inflections, but he wondered why Mathew was in such a hurry to move into the negotiation.

Esteban leaned back in his chair, reached up and stroked away the sweat that was beading beneath his mustache, "I can be very useful to your government. I know things."

"We already know things, more things than you can possibly imagine," Mathew said.

"You only think you know. I've been smuggling drugs, weapons, and people into your country for thirty years, and less than two percent of my shipments have been seized. You think you know so much? You don't know shit!"

He leaned aggressively forward over his desk, "If these people get their way, they are going to flood the United States with the deadliest drug you've ever seen. So much that there isn't enough money to hire all the cops it would take to police it. You think the opioid addiction problem your president is ranting about now is a problem? This will kill more Americans than a nuclear war."

"And you're willing to give us the information to stop these people? Everything - names, dates, places, maps, bank accounts. Everything?"

"Yes."

"So, back to my original question. What do you want?"

"First, full immunity in writing, from prosecution for anything I might have ever done. And, I want to live in West Palm Beach. My sister lives there, and there are a lot of exiled people from my country, so I can have friends. I want citizenship for myself and my daughter, and I want full access to banks accounts I have anywhere in the world, without taxes."

"That's asking a lot, Esteban." Mathew turned and looked at Diggs, as if trying to get him into the game. But Diggs remained quiet.

"Give us something right now. Give us a sample of what we'll be paying for, and I'll take it up the chain."

Esteban stood up from his chair quickly, and Diggs reflexively slid his right hand back to where the handle of his Glock would have been. The spot was still warm from the gun rubbing against his waist. Esteban's eyes picked up the movement and he froze, "Easy my friend, I'm just stretching my legs."

"Let's get something straight. I'm not your friend." Diggs said.

"Alright, alright. Be calm," Esteban said. He turned to the window and looked out over the long green pasture behind his house. A beautiful black horse was grazing at the far end, and he could see the Caribbean Sea beyond. "That's my daughter's horse. She loves that horse more than she loves me. We should bring that horse to West Palm too."

Then he turned around and looked at Mathew, "The Cubans have convinced the Venezuelan government to get back into the drug business. They want to produce a very addictive drug made from fentanyl and opium, just like what the Chinese and the Mexicans are doing, only far more potent."

Mathew interjected, "The Venezuelan government doesn't have the resources to handle it. Who else is involved? Who is supplying the opium?"

"The Arabs. The Russians are willing to finance the laboratory and the chemical engineers to make the drugs. They figure, since the Chinese are getting rich from selling it in the USA, then they might as well make some too, and weaken the imperialists in the bargain."

Diggs again kept his eyes on Esteban, and he saw them flicker nervously to him, then back to Mathew.

"The Arabs are bringing the opium in another week or so, and the Russians are paying for the first shipment up front. $1.2 billion dollars' worth. After that, they might partner in for a percentage. Venezuela will make money, the Arabs will make money for their little wars against the Jews, and the cartels will make more money on their girls."

"Girls?" Diggs said.

"Yes, the Arabs are going to guarantee a market for a minimum of five thousand girls a year from the Central American cartels.

The girls have an expected value of eighty-thousand dollars each for their working life, and the Arabs will pay twenty-thousand dollars cash for each, if they meet their standards. That's another guaranteed annual income of one-hundred million dollars to the cartels. Not a bad sideline business. The

Cubans are going to send back a free sample of half a dozen girls with the emissary."

Diggs asked, "Were these the girls taken last month in Barcelona? Where are they now?"

"I don't know for certain, but I suspect they are on the island of Curaçao. That's where they are meeting the Arabs to transfer the opium and the money. Bram Bay has been a hub for smugglers for two hundred years. It's possible they have the girls there as well, so they can hand them over at the same time."

"And your daughter, Camila, is she with them?"

"I pray to the Virgin Mother, not. The girls who are taken, taken to be sold ... are not well treated. They need to be conditioned for their new life."

"Sounds like you're very familiar with the process, Esteban," Diggs said. His typically stoic projection was beginning crack, and his hatred hovering beneath a very thin veil of self-control.

Esteban stared back, and the corners of his mouth twisted inward. "Are you going to judge me? You? The man who has famously murdered his way across the entire world, under the banner of the CIA? The things I've done in my life to feed my family and support my country pale in comparison to you. I know who you are, William Diggs. I remember you from the old days."

"Yes, and I remember you too, *Butcher*."

Mathew stood up quickly and stepped between the two men. It was a dangerous place to be. On one side, an ex-socialist revolutionary turned cartel boss, and on the other, an old-school CIA assassin. "Let's try to stay focused on the present gentlemen. No need to fight the old wars all over again."

Diggs collected himself and sat back down. Then he came straight out with it, "Why would the Cubans want to kill Mariella Martinez?"

Esteban looked dumbfounded for a moment. He looked to Mathew, as if he might bail him out, then back to Diggs.

"Martinez was a spy. The Cubans had been looking for her for years. I guess they finally found her."

Now Diggs was calculating how he could escape the estancia compound after he killed Esteban. There was a heavy glass ashtray on the edge of the desk. It would easily smash Esteban's skull. But getting out of here alive might not be possible.

Then he thought about Lucas, Eliza, and the young girls trapped somewhere and terrified. He knew he had to just wait it out. There would be another time to kill Esteban, and he would take his time.

32

Lucas had rented a bungalow at the Van der Koost, a very private little boutique hotel that was nestled on a man-made peninsula outside Willemstad, to use as a base while he conducted daily reconnaissance of the bank and surrounding locations. He was sitting on the open lanai, sipping a very bitter Dutch coffee and listening to the light lapping of waves against the concrete walls of the jetty. He heard a single knock on the door.

"It's open," he said.

"Leaving your door unlocked and inviting the world in? My training has already worn off on you," Diggs said as he entered.

"It hasn't worn off. This hotel can only be accessed through the main drive and front lobby. I put your tradecraft to good use. I made friends with the young girl at the front desk and bribed her to call me if anyone new showed up. She gave me a warning a few minutes ago, with your description."

Diggs smiled. "Where did you leave Serge?"

"He is sleeping in the jet. He doesn't want to leave his stash of weapons unattended."

Diggs sat down at the glass-topped table just inside the sliding doors and motioned for Lucas to come in, away from the prying eyes and satellites that are constantly hovering overhead. "I have good intel on the plans and players involved, where the exchanges are happening with the opium, and very likely where the girls are being held captive."

He pulled a plain manila envelope from the canvas messenger bag and lay out a series of black and white images taken from the edge of space. Lucas came in and sat beside him.

"There's regular small boat traffic coming from the coast of Venezuela to Curaçao almost every day, mostly fisherman making the journey across to sell their catch for twenty times more than they could get for it at home. But several weeks ago, there was a larger vessel that left from a remote beach-head outside the town of Barcelona at midnight, and it sailed directly to the port of Bram Bay. It was just a few hours after a van loaded with schoolgirls was ambushed, and the girls abducted."

"You think the girls are still being held there?"

"No. We think they were being held in these two

shipping containers," as he pointed to them on the photographs. "But yesterday these images were taken." The second set of satellite photos appeared to show several armed men carrying five smaller females out of the containers and loading them into a van. "They took them to a large house on the coast just a short drive away. They are probably cleaning the girls up for delivery. Our intelligence is telling us now, that the girls are going to be transferred to the yacht and sent to the Middle East, after the opium is offloaded at Bram Bay and sent into Venezuela."

"Can I ask where you came by this intel?"

"The CIA Station Chief in Caracas called me. It would take too much time for me to explain all of the history here, but suffice to say, an old military colonel has resurfaced. He's neck deep in this, and he's trying to switch sides. His daughter was one of those taken, and he wants to cut a deal for asylum, and our help getting her back."

Lucas could tell that something was different about Diggs this time. His normal manner, the stoic, emotionless face and eyes that were so black to be nearly void of color were somehow different. Now he could see the hints of stress. Faint lines etched across his forehead, and the warm glow of veins surrounding the dark iris. There was something very deep and personal about this for his mentor.

"There are a lot of moving pieces here. How are we going to take out the emissary, capture the financier, and rescue these girls? We're a little short on manpower."

"The emissary, his name is Aziz Harrak, is going to transfer the opium in the morning. We need to let him complete that delivery, and then communicate back to his handlers that it's done, and primary money transfer is completed. They'll be waiting on the call.

After that they won't be expecting to hear from him again until after the financier has moved the cash into other accounts they can draw from, which won't be until the next business day. Avigail will travel with him to Willemstad, and my friends with the Mossad will take possession of Aziz somewhere along the route. They are eager to ask him questions about the Beirut connections. The Israelis always have questions."

Lucas was already uncomfortable with the plan, "I don't want Avi in the middle of this, it's not safe."

"Avigail will be fine, she has put herself in very dangerous situations before. Don't forget, she made herself a part of this little private war and nearly got both of us killed in Mallorca. She owes us, so let her do her part."

"So the Mossad are going to take out the emissary before he arrives in Willemstad, and I take his place from there?"

"Yes. And Avigail will go to the bank with you. No one seems to know who this mystery banker is, but it's possible she has met him before if he comes from Farouk Kateb's old group, and she might recognize him."

"And the girls?"

"The girls are probably being detoxed and cleaned up right now. We think they won't try to move them until after the dope and money have all changed hands. We should be able to snatch the emissary and the banker in the afternoon and take them underground. Then hit the house where the girls are being held before sunrise the next morning."

"How many guards at the house? Can we handle it with just you, me, and Serge on overwatch?

"There are only four roving guards who come and go at regular times in the morning and afternoon. Shouldn't be a problem."

33

Aziz stood naked in front of the full-length mirror in his stateroom, feeling slightly nauseous from the light rolling of the yacht in the eastern swell. Looking into the mirror made it worse. He abandoned his morning ritual of watching himself as he masturbated, and ran into the bathroom to vomit.

When he finished, he leaned over the sink and splashed his mouth and face with cool water, then stood staring into the small round mirror on the wall. The voyage across the Atlantic had been a misery for him. Not having spent any time on the sea, he was nearly constantly sick, and worse yet, Avigail had rebuffed all of his attempts to have sex. The second day at sea, she confined herself to her stateroom; and when he tried to force his way in, that woman, the Sultana, had intervened.

Eliza and her constantly hovering bodyguards drove him away from Avigail's door. "She is not in any condition to attend to you now. You must leave her alone," the Sultana had told him. When he demanded to know why, she said, "It is customary for a woman to remain isolated during her monthly condition." Which angered him even more that she would share such information with him. If it weren't for her guards standing next to her, he would have beaten her for her insolence.

He had been counting on having Avigail at his pleasure for the entire week of travel aboard the yacht. It was the only reason he allowed her to come along. The frustration was killing him, and his lack of authority aboard this vessel was pissing him off. He felt weak and ignored among the crew and guards that attended to every wish of the Sultana. But that was about to change.

He could already feel the subtle slowing of the enormous turbine engines below the decks and the yacht beginning its pitch to an anchorage. They were only a few miles off the shore of Curaçao, and soon, very soon, he would be in charge of everything again.

He would use the satellite phone to advise his superiors in Beirut that he had arrived successfully in time, with the cargo. He would deliver it early tomorrow morning, and he would verify the bank accounts with the financier from Gibraltar.

Then, he would do whatever he wanted with

Avigail, and if she didn't please him, he would kill her and dump her body in the sea.

THE YACHT WAS SECURED by three anchor lines, keeping her bow into the constant waves that flowed from the east, and her stern aimed squarely at the commercial port of Bram Bay. The bay was a twenty minute boat ride from Willemstad, where he had to meet the financier, but this is where the Cubans had requested the transfer of the opium take place, far from any prying eyes.

AZIZ REMOVED the satellite phone from his leather travel bag and made a call to Beirut.

"I have arrived in Curaçao and will deliver the product tomorrow, then verify the transfer of funds, Your Highness," he said, …"Yes, Your Highness, I understand the instructions very clearly. When the funds have been dispersed as you have ordered, I will complete the business here with the woman, then begin the journey back to Marrakech." He was unaware that his call was being monitored.

Aziz recovered from his sea-sickness and he walked out onto the salon-level deck that faced the shore. He was surprised to see Avigail lounging on a cushioned chair in the sun, and though he was disgusted by how immodestly she was dressed; he desired her all the more. "You are suddenly well enough to enjoy the outdoors. How fortunate."

She was wearing a very revealing white bathing suit that contrasted with her Mediterranean tan and flowing black hair. She was lying shifted to one side, and her breasts were trying to break loose from the confines of the sheer fabric. She was looking down at a book in her left hand, and without moving her head up to face him directly, she reached up with a finger and slid her sunglasses down an inch, peering at him over the rim.

Her condescending glance enraged him. "I'm growing tired of you woman! Be dressed more appropriately tomorrow, and ready to leave with me very early. I'm taking you with me to the city. Being on this yacht with the Sultana has corrupted you!"

34

Raphael had left the house early, along with his Russian companion, and even though it was still dark outside, the house was buzzing with activity. Men moving up and down the staircase from the basement, the housekeeper hustling in the kitchen, and Camila too was awake upstairs.

Outside at the seawall an older man with long gray hair pulled into a pony tail stood at the end of the dock under a yellow halogen lamp post, a few random moths flapping in circles above his head. He was wearing fashionable jeans, expensive deck shoes, a black silk shirt, and he watched as two men struggled to carry a slender steel crate down from the big blue house. On the second floor, he saw a pretty young girl standing in the window, also watching intently.

His cell phone rang. He looked at the caller ID and touched the green button.

. . .

"Antonio, are you ready to start your run?"

"Almost. The guards are loading the final two crates now."

"And the other package?"

"The other package is prepared and will be loaded just before launch."

"Excellent. You know exactly where I will meet you, yes?"

"Si Señor."

"This run will set you free, Antonio. Your life will be your own after this is done. And one more thing, Antonio … I'll be watching you."

The call ended.

Tethered on a rope leash against the dock, faintly rocking from side to side in the rising tide, was a long rapier-looking boat. A brand new fifty-nine foot Tirranna ocean racer, shaped like a missile, and nearly as fast. Repainted in flat black with a low-radar-signature paint, she was reminiscent of the cigarette racers of old, only powered by six, fuel gobbling, 400 HP Mercury Verado Racing engines.

Built for nothing but speed on the open ocean, the Tirranna could reach sixty miles per hour in rough water and hold enough fuel to run for nearly eight-hundred nautical miles at a cruising speed of forty three knots. This particular boat had been modified to hold another four-hundred gallons, which meant she could make the run from the Venezuelan coast to the US mainland in one fast bolt across the open Caribbean, skirting the Cuban coastline.

Antonio watched the final crate being loaded and secured into the smuggler's hull, behind the main sleeping berth. Each of the crates, sixteen in all, were filled with certified "Good Delivery", one kilo gold bars, approximately one-hundred and thirty million dollars' worth. Totaling just over two tons, the crates had to be evenly distributed along the balance line of the hull, or the boat wouldn't handle predictably. She might wallow or yaw in a big sea, and at full speed, that could mean the difference between living or dying.

He stepped down over the crates, spread his feet to their full reach outward, and shifted his weight back and forth to feel how she pitched under the load. "Move the crates on the left over three inches, and the two back crates forward two inches," he said to the guards loading them. They obeyed his explicit instructions. They knew that onboard the boat, Antonio's word was law.

He tested the action once again, and satisfied, gave the thumbs up to strap the crates tightly with locking ratchets. Once secured, they wouldn't budge, even in a high-speed race over crashing swells.

Antonio Barrow was once a king. The figurative king of Thunder Boat Row. In the 1970s and 80s, Miami, Florida, was the epicenter of the hottest new racing scene in the world, the birthplace of offshore cigarette boat racing. The rich, the royal, and the beautiful of the sporting world all gathered at the end of Miami Avenue to worship at the altar of speed, and Antonio was the fastest of them all.

The son of a Cuban mother and Argentinian father, he was a bronzed sea god, chiseled by surf, sun, and dangerous living. Rich men around the world paid any price to have Antonio behind the wheel and throttles of their million-dollar boats. His success as a racer made their boats famous, and the owners of famous racing boats were engulfed in fame of their own. And as rich men paid Antonio for speed, rich women often paid Antonio for his prowess in the berth. As the saying goes, every woman wanted him, and every man wanted to be him.

There are two varieties of men drawn to offshore boat racing; the crazy and the fearless. Antonio was fearless. But it was the rare combination of courage, talent, and the ability to accurately assess risk that kept Antonio alive for so many years in a sport that claimed the lives of many.

But all things pass away, in time. The rich of the world eventually became bored with watching their boats roaring across the finish line with someone else at the wheel. Thunder Boat Row dwindled and vanished into the history books of hot locales. Antonio Barrow relinquished his throne and had to find a new way to make a living. Fortunately for him, as the Miami racing scene was winding down, the smuggling scene was just getting started.

All manner of elicit things were being transported from Central America to the United States. At first, in small quantities that were easily packed in a suitcase aboard a commercial aircraft. But as demand increased and enforcement became more serious, other means had to be found, and a man with Antonio's skillsets suddenly became valuable again.

A fast cigarette boat with extra fuel tanks for extended runs could navigate under the radar, weaving between the myriad of islands and islets of the Caribbean, under the cover of darkness, and deliver cargo up to a few thousand pounds without sacrificing much in the way of speed.

Given his heritage, Antonio was embraced by the cartels of Colombia and Venezuela. He was discrete, reliable, spoke Spanish and English fluently, and with a properly outfitted boat, he was nearly uncatchable on the open water. A few times over the years, he had been tracked by regional law enforcement, and even the US Coast Guard twice, but had never been caught. The only time anyone came close was when he was pursued by a DEA helicopter, and he cleverly ducked under the safety of Cuban airspace to escape.

Now at the age of sixty-two, Antonio's face was no longer as handsome and chiseled as it once was. His skin had lost the smooth bronzed sheen, and more closely resembled an aging leather armchair left too long near the south-facing window; it was dried to brownish black and spider-webbed with cracks and fissures. His eyes were permanently narrowed by decades of squinting into the sun and sparkling reflections of the sea. Even though much of his working hours were now spent in the darkness, his skin had never returned to its youthful luster.

But he was still fierce behind the wheel and throttles.

RAPHAEL HAD ARRANGED for Antonio to transport the ten percent royalty owed to the Cuban Intelligence Directorate and paid by the Venezuelan government in gold. His run would take him directly north between the islands of Haiti and Jamaica, to the safety of Cuban territorial waters. Then he would follow the coast of Cuba around the eastern side to Port Matanzas. A contingent of military and DI officials would be waiting for him to unload and take the gold to the underground vaults at Camp Matanzas.

A sizable sum would be waiting for Antonio in his bank account in Miami, which is where he wanted to spend his final years; fishing, drinking, and lusting after young women. He had dreams of recapturing his youth in the clubs along the Miami marina row and South Beach.

Given his departure time and the forecast of calm seas, he anticipated reaching his final destination just before dawn of the next day.

Antonio stepped into the pilot's cockpit and began his pre-trip checks. There were two 24 inch monitors over the helm, one which displayed a constant Garmin GPS Satellite image, the other had digital displays of engine data, temperatures, fuel consumption, and more. Nine additional smaller displays were scattered about the cockpit.

One by one, he toggled open the ignition switches and started each engine, watching the fuel vacuum gauges and oil temperature rise and settle as they warmed up. By the time all six were running, the echoes from the engines at idle against the bulkhead sounded like the starting line at the Grand Prix of Monaco.

He turned to the guard standing outside the back door of the house and motioned for the final package to be loaded. A minute later, the guard came walking down the dock, carrying a small pink suitcase, with Camila Aguera walking beside him.

Antonio reached and took the suitcase, then held

up his hand to Camila to help her into the boat. She hesitated.

"Come along, Señorita. We have a long trip ahead of us."

"I'm afraid," she said.

"You have nothing to be afraid of. I am the most famous racing boat driver in all the world, and this is a very safe boat. You will have your very own cabin below the deck, with a comfortable bed, so you can sleep the whole way if you want to." He nodded to the guard standing behind her, and the man gave Camila a slight nudge to force her over the gunwale. She squealed as she fell forward, but Antonio caught her in his arms.

"There, you see, nothing to it. Now go below through that pretty teakwood door and go to sleep. I'll wake you when we arrive at your new home."

Camila stepped through the door, and into the elegantly decorated berth, with a king-sized bed, and a small private bathroom. As she went in and put her suitcase on the bed, the door slammed closed behind her and the latch bolted shut from the outside. For the second time since being kidnapped, she was trapped in a small confined space.

Antonio untied the tether line and threw it up to the guard, "Will you be in Matanzas with Raphael?"

"No, he is flying to Cuba later today in a Cessna. I have to stay here until the other girls are delivered out to the Arabs."

"Ok then, tell Raphael I'll see him in about twenty hours."

He placed his right hand around the two throttle levers, each operating three engines, and bumped them upward. The rhythmic thumping of the idle turned into a steady drone as the big boat moved ahead. He pushed the throttles further, and where he would normally feel the long piercing bow of the Tirranna rising, instead she plowed deep through the water under the load of two tons of gold in her belly.

Finally, he pushed them to the stops and with a massive howl, the boat jumped forward, and then eased over into a racing trim atop the water. In only moments, she was slicing over the glassy Caribbean at about 50 knots and vanishing to the horizon.

35

Aziz had been standing alone on the foredeck since 4:00 a.m., waiting for the sun to rise on his day of ultimate triumph. He was going to seal the alliance between Hezbollah and their new partners, and personally oversee the delivery of opium and the transfer of over a billion dollars for the benefit of holy jihad.

When the stars on the western horizon began to disappear into a gray sky, he ordered the crew to pull the pallets up from below deck and load them onto the motor launch. He wasn't going to miss his 6:30 meeting on the dock at Bram Bay.

Avigail would accompany him for the meeting with the South Americans. Even though he had no real need for her assistance, he wanted to show that he was man of power and status, with a beautiful woman waiting to serve his needs. And, it would be the first time in a week that he would have her alone and away from the Sultana and her guards. If he felt like touching her, he would. If he wanted to take her forcefully, no one could stop him. Then, if he decided she no longer pleased him and he wanted to kill her, he could do that too.

She came out onto the landing deck of the yacht, wearing a crimson dress that showed far too much of her stunning legs, and was cut deeply in front to reveal an emerald pendant nestled between her breasts. Her long black hair was loosely braided and pulled around over her left shoulder, to keep it from tangling in the wind and surf during the ride in the smaller motor launch to shore.

She wore comfortable deck shoes for getting in and out of the boat and had a pair of Christian Louboutin heels tucked away in a stylish carry bag to change into for the venture into Willemstad. This wasn't Avigail's first time to function as adornment for a self-aggrandizing man.

The driver offered up his hand as she balanced a foot on the gunwale, then she lowered herself gracefully onto the comfortable seating that wrapped around the rear of the boat. Aziz paid no attention to her arrival. He stood tall in front of the open windscreen, like a rooster proclaiming his domain. The two pallets of opium were tied down on the open deck in front of him.

The driver threw off the bow line, then pulled

away from the towering yacht and throttled up towards the shore of Bram Bay on the near horizon. Eliza was standing along the railing of the third level deck below the helipad, watching their departure.

The breeze blew lightly from the west this morning, and the launch rolled up and down, sending a crisp spray of green sea over the gunwales. "Not so fast, you idiot! You are going to wet the pallets, and you have no idea how valuable those are!" he screamed at the boat driver.

He exchanged a glance with Avigail but didn't speak. She smiled demurely, and took refuge in the knowledge that Aziz's time was about to come.

As they neared the bay, Aziz could see the long pier stretching out over two hundred yards from the shore to the deep-water moorings, and at the end of the pier, two men, one short and dark, the other tall and blonde. Behind them, two men with machine-guns standing guard, and two more waiting where the pier jutted into the white sandy beach.

Near the end of the pier, a large crusty looking fishing boat was tied up, and as the motor launch approached, the men signaled to park up next to it. "Just stay where you are, and don't speak," Aziz said to Avigail and the driver as they came up to the pier. "I'm the only one with authority here."

The boat driver expertly maneuvered the launch up next to the fishing boat, and two dirty looking men threw over a rope to the bow and another to the stern to secure the two boats together. Aziz stepped over the pallets and up onto the pier, "I am Aziz Harrak, the emissary," he proudly announced.

The short dark-haired man stepped forward with a brilliant smile, "My name is Raphael. We are very happy to receive you here on our side of the world," he said as he reached out his hand. "We believe this will be a very profitable alliance for all of our people."

The tall, pale man in a black linen shirt and jeans said something in Russian.

Raphael translated, "My Russian friend would like to sample and test the opium before we move it to our boat, and when he is satisfied with the quality, he will approve the wire transfer of payment."

Aziz was used to dealing with Spaniards and French, and sometimes Belgians, but they were not so intimidating as this enormous Russian. He turned and waved his hand toward the drugs. The Russian stepped onto the bow of the motor launch, and pulled three glass vials from his shirt pocket, and a long slender knife from his waistband.

The pallets each contained two-hundred and fifty wrapped kilos inside the boxes labeled as tangerines. He randomly selected a box from the top and one from the middle of the first pallet, and one from the bottom of the second. He slit the cardboard tops open and then pierced the wrapped bags of opium with the blade, retrieving a small crusty sample from each and depositing them into the vials.

He touched the residue on the blade to the tip of his tongue, and his eye twitched as the satisfyingly bitter taste reached the back of his throat. He hocked the minuscule amount back up and spat it out and nodded his head, signifying it had the strong alkaloid taste he would have expected. Then he held all three vials together and pulled out a small jar with an eye-dropper and placed five drops of clear liquid into each.

Then, one by one, he covered the open vials with his fingertip and shook them vigorously for a few seconds. The residue in each turned a brilliant magenta color. He turned to Raphael, "Da." Then he motioned for the two dirty men in the fishing boat to begin transferring the cases of "tangerines."

"Wait," Aziz said. "Not until the money has been wired."

Raphael said something in Russian to his compatriot. The big man tipped his head and smirked at Aziz. He stepped back onto the pier and one of the guards handed him a tablet, which he opened and began tapping a series of entries on the screen keyboard. Then he closed it and nodded his head again.

Aziz now took out his satellite phone and called the number he had been given by his handler in Beirut. It clicked three times, then began to ring to another cell phone. A man answered, "This is Constantino. Who is speaking?"

"I am Aziz. Please confirm the transfer has been completed."

"One moment," he said. "Yes. The transfer is complete. I will be at the bank in Willemstad waiting for your arrival."

Aziz folded down the antenna on the phone and slipped it back into his pocket, then he turned to Raphael, "Everything is done, your men can transfer the boxes."

Raphael smiled and motioned to the men to move over the cargo. "I have arranged for a car and driver to be at your service during your stay in Curaçao. I assume you will want to meet your financier at the Royal Ingstedt Bank in Willemstad first."

Aziz was suddenly wondering how the Cuban knew about Constantino's arrival. "Yes, I will be going to Willemstad, but our boat driver is going to take us directly to the port. It is only a twenty minute ride and the sea is very pleasant today." Then he changed the subject, "I was told that I will be returning to Morocco with samples as well."

"Samples? Ah, yes. You mean the young ladies. They are being prepared for travel as we speak, but we need a bit more time. It's a stressful process for them. I'm sure you understand what I mean. You should take the day to enjoy the sights of Curaçao, and I will have them delivered to your yacht tomorrow afternoon. I think you will be pleased with the selection of beautiful young Latina girls, and it is an endless resource."

"I hope so. The men in our countries have a great appetite for beautiful women," he said. Then he turned and smiled at Avigail. She appeared bored with the entire business, as though she were more interested in the shorebirds that swooped and dipped at the surface of the water, but she was listening intently to every word spoken.

36

The boat ride at full speed along the southern shoreline of Curaçao, was only twenty minutes to the capital of Willemstad. But Aziz's frustrations with Avigail's lack of female attentiveness had reached a fevered pitch, and now that he had her all alone he intended to have his way.

They were riding on a glassy surface, within two-hundred yards of the palm-lined shore, when Aziz leaned over to the boat driver, "Keep your eyes on the sea ahead, my friend. I have some business with the woman." The boat driver smiled and nodded his head.

Aziz walked back to the lounge seating in the stern of the boat and fell back into the cushion with a sigh. "I've just negotiated the greatest alliance in the history of my people. I deserve to be rewarded," he said. Then he reached over and slid his hand aggressively into the top of Avigail's dress and clutched her breast.

Avigail tried to hold her composure. She had feared that he might try to force himself on her somewhere during the trip to Willemstad. "Aziz, I desire you too, but can't you wait just a few hours longer. Here on this filthy boat, with a stranger only feet away from us, isn't the place I would prefer to make love to you for the first time."

"I don't give a shit what you prefer! I've had enough of your teasing, and the Sultana hounding me to stay away from you. You're going to give me what I want now, or I'll throw your pretty ass into the sea for the sharks!" Then he stood up and towered over her, and slapped her violently across the face, knocking her over onto the lounge.

She looked up and stared into his eyes, but not with the look he had anticipated. She wasn't afraid, or prepared to give in to his wishes. Her green eyes were glazed over into a storm cloud of anger, like a deadly viper about to molt its old worthless skin and rise anew.

The outline of his hand was burning red on her cheek, and the stinging sensation awakened her deepest emotions. This wasn't the first, or even the hundredth time a man had left his mark on her, but it was going to be the last.

She came back up quickly, and as she rose, she reached out for his crotch. She easily found his testicles through the light linen slacks, and she grabbed them and jerked down as hard as she could. Aziz shrieked like a little girl, as Avigail pulled and snatched his manhood from one side to the other. Then he fell forward onto his knees and clutched her forearm, but he hadn't the strength to pry her grip loose.

She held firm with her assaulting hand and ground the sharpened thumbnail of her other hand into his right eye socket, which made him collapse backward onto the teakwood deck of the boat. She came with him, sitting astride his thighs, and reached down now with her free hand to reinforce the vice grip she had and squeezed even harder.

Aziz screamed at the top of his lungs now, his wailing echoing across the faraway waterfront. Then out of nowhere, a heavy wooden oar handle came smashing down across his forehead, and the wailing ceased.

Avigail didn't seem to notice for an instant. She kept on crushing him in her hands, oblivious to the fact that Aziz was no longer conscious. Then she looked up and saw the boat driver, standing over them with the oar.

"Eli told me you would do what needed to be done to maintain the mission, but he also told me not to let anyone hurt you," he said in Hebrew.

"I was hurting him, not the other way around."

"Yes, I can see that now. Please forgive me for

intruding in the lover's quarrel, but his screaming was going to attract attention if it went on much longer."

AVIGAIL GOT TO HER FEET, standing over Aziz's limp form, and spat on him. Then she walked forward to the windscreen of the boat and looked ahead across the brilliant blue water. The channel entrance to Willemstad was only a few miles further.

"We need to tie him up securely and store him under the deck. If anyone sees him while we're coming into the port, they might call the police."

They took a long length of rope that was coiled on the foredeck and bound the body like a hog for slaughter. Then the driver pulled up the deck panels to reveal the storage compartments below, and they rolled his body down into it. Avigail pulled a dirty rag from the mechanic's box in the hold and shoved it deep into his throat. "Just in case he wakes up. We don't want him making any noise."

"Go through his pockets and get the sat-phone, and see if he has his passport. If he and Lucas resemble each other enough, it might be useful," the Israeli driver said.

37

Lucas was standing with his back to the pier, trying to occupy his mind with the old Dutch buildings lined across the waterfront. They were odd, square, nearly formless and void of any character, save for the vibrant colors they were painted. The colors reminded him of the city where he and Eliza were raised, Barcelona, Spain, but the architecture here was so plain and boringly functional.

He could hear the launch coming down the channel behind him, but he hesitated to turn and face her.

It was the great mystery that perplexed him and being perplexed made him afraid. The man who fears nothing, but he was afraid of her. He was afraid of the power she seemed to have over him.

. . .

From the moment he first saw her in Monte Carlo, she struck a chord of terror inside him. The trained killer, assassin, the man who had sought out the most dangerous assignments that might offer him the chance to die a glorious death, and yet, the first vision of this woman had changed him. He still didn't fear death, but he feared a life without Avigail being a part of it.

They were in each other's company only a few days, but in those days, she saved his life, he saved hers, he experienced true love, and utter betrayal. He had never known a woman. Avigail had known many men, but never one that she had chosen herself. She also fell deeply in love, and then she did what she had been programmed to do and sent him to die. Then in sorrow and desperation, she threw herself into the sea.

Lucas took a deep breath and turned, just as the motor launch thumped against the rubber cushions on the landing dock. Avigail was standing on the very edge of the bow, eager to leave the boat, in part perhaps because of what had transpired with Aziz only fifteen minutes before. But also because seeing Lucas' unmistakable form on the landing, growing closer with each passing second, had stirred the same emotions. She feared him, and she was desperate to see him.

In the crimson red dress, she looked very much like the first time, which was how he continued to imagine her in his mind. He walked forward to the edge and reached out to her, and when their hands touched, he felt the same searing heat in his palm as he had felt the first time her naked body pressed against him.

Any anger, or animosity, or fear he might have still harbored, vanished in the blink of an eye.

As she stepped onto the dock, his heart took complete control, and he pulled her close.

"Avi, you look … you look just like I've seen you in my mind."

She smiled, pulled off her large sunglasses and leaned into him, "I wasn't sure you wanted to see me."

He looked in her eyes, now warmed to the glowing emerald color they had when she was happy, then he noticed the pink residue of Aziz's slap on the side of her face.

"What happened to your face?" he said. Then he realized that in his absorption with Avigail, he had forgotten that the emissary, Aziz, was supposed to arrive with her. "Did that Moroccan bastard hurt you? I'll kill him!"

The boat driver spoke from behind them, "You don't need to worry about her, Lucas. She can handle herself. In fact, she fairly well kicked the shit out of the Moroccan. I had to put him out of his misery to stop his crying."

"Who are you?" Lucas said.

"My name is Gabe. I work for Eli Moskarov. Aziz is tucked away safely under here," he said, pointing to the deck of the boat.

"Is he still alive?"

"For now. Eli thinks he might prove useful."

Lucas looked at Avigail, "I'm sorry they dragged you into this. I would have never wanted it."

"I wanted to be here, Lucas. I'm only here for you."

Lucas and Avigail walked along the waterfront to a small cafe where they could see the entrance to the Royal Ingstedt Bank, and took a table outside on the breezeway.

"I am supposed to meet the financier from Gibraltar, or rather, Aziz is supposed to meet him, in exactly two hours. We'll keep watch from here."

"I brought Aziz's passport, just in case you need it. You are much more handsome than he is, but you both have very dark skin and hair and are about the same age. The quality of the passport photograph is so terrible that no one would probably even question it."

Gabe, the Israeli Mossad agent posing as a launch operator, moved the boat to a more private area of the marina and tied it securely. Then he started walking around the three blocks surrounding the bank, entering a few shops and making small purchases, and taking a series of videos of everyone on the streets with a discrete camera that was automatically uploading the files via his cell phone, to an internet server.

Within minutes of being uploaded, a team of agents in a crowded little office in Tel Aviv were scouring the videos and running them through facial recognition software. They were worried that the Islamists might have sent more agents than just Aziz, without telling him. After all, they had a great deal riding on this alliance.

38

WILLEMSTAD, CURAÇAO

Gabe walked up to the cafe where Lucas and Avigail were seated outside, and he took a chair at an empty table that backed up to Lucas, facing away. He placed his shopping bags in the opposite chair and motioned for the waiter. A young girl wearing a bright orange apron, the Dutch national colors, walked over, laid a menu down in front of him and asked, "Would you like something to drink, sir?"

"Bottled water, please. Perrier if you have it."

After the waiter walked away, he opened the menu and feigned interest, then spoke just barely loud enough for Lucas to hear, "Our team has been watching the banker, Constantino Gallo, since he arrived yesterday. He just left his hotel and should be arriving here within ten minutes. I'll point him out when he gets here." Lucas kept his gaze focused entirely on Avigail, which wasn't difficult, and made no signs that he heard.

AVIGAIL WAS SEATED with her back to the water, where she could see both directly into Lucas' eyes, and also beyond to the entrance of the bank and the street in front. She saw the man, just as Gabe whispered, "There he is."

Sixty-ish, slender and tall, handsome, with dark hair that was pure silver in the temples. He was wearing a dark tailored suit like a typical European, which made him stand out like a sore thumb in the Caribbean, and carrying a black leather attaché case with a thin wire cable secured tightly around his wrist.

Lucas watched as the delicate lines that framed the corners of Avigail's mouth when she was smiling, suddenly tensed and furrowed as the smile collapsed and her lower lip fell slightly open. Her eyes were frozen wide, then blinked rapidly twice, and her head made a subconscious jerk as if she had gone into a trance for a moment, then snapped awake. She looked frightened. More than frightened. Terrified, like she had just seen a ghost.

Lucas fought the urge to spin around to see what she was seeing, and remained facing her, "What is it? What are you seeing?"

She opened her mouth but couldn't speak. She closed her lips tightly and rolled them over each other and dampened them with her tongue. "I know this man," she said as she shifted her eyes to Lucas.

He could see the fear in her face. "Who is he?"

"His name isn't Constantino Gallo," she said, shifting her eyes back to the man walking across the street. "His name is … Francisco Martell."

Lucas leaned toward her like he was about to ask her to repeat what she had said, and just as he was about to stand and turn around, she reached across the table and put her hand on his arm, "Don't turn around. He might not be alone, and he might not be happy to see you."

Lucas was stunned. "Are you telling me my father, my father who died four months ago in Monaco, is walking across the street behind me? That my father is the new banker for the Islamic terrorist mafia?"

As the words were coming out of his mouth, he was flashing backward in his mind.

He had been determined to see the actual place where his father died in a car crash, the steep cliffside above the Mediterranean Sea in the small Village of Cap-d' Ail on the coast of Monaco. He remembered the strange little constable who took him to the site of the crash and told him the story of how the car lost control and went over the edge.

Lucas had stood looking down the near vertical drop-off. He could see the scars in the earth and rocks, and gouges made by the tumbling steel wreckage of the Mercedes limousine, and the patches of blackened and scorched grass where it came to rest.

He also remembered looking closely at the twisting tire marks still seared into the pavement, and thinking at that moment, *Something isn't right.* Then he recalled what Avigail had told him later, that Francisco was never supposed to be going to Cap-d' Ail that night, that it shouldn't have happened, and no one had a good explanation.

As stunning as it was to hear that his father was alive and walking across the street behind him, Lucas was not entirely surprised. He couldn't explain why his father might be here at this moment, or how he might be involved with the Arabs, but to learn that he was alive suddenly felt plausible. Like he had known it deep inside for a long time.

THE MOSSAD AGENT, Gabe, tensed in his chair as he was also about to spin around and face Lucas. He whispered low, "Avigail, are you sure?"

"Yes, I worked with him for years, and I spoke to

him the day he died. Or, the day we all thought he died." She looked back at Lucas, "I'm sorry, I don't know what to say. But, it is definitely Francisco."

Lucas' mind was spinning now. His father had been in hiding under a new identity, and obviously taken over as the banker for the criminal enterprises immediately after Lucas killed his old boss, Jean-Étienne Berger. Could Francisco have been a part of it all along? Did he fake his own death? After all, the constable in Cap-d' Ail said the body in the back seat was burned beyond recognition, and they just assumed it to be Francisco Martell.

Had Francisco been plotting to take over the banking and money-laundering for terrorists, drug lords, and human traffickers?

"*And I handed him the keys to the kingdom when I killed Berger and all of his security team,*" Lucas thought.

Then the worst scenario of all came to the front of Lucas' mind. Could his father have had something to do with the kidnapping of his own daughter, Eliza?

Lucas' face went blank. He had the same stoic stare as his mentor-in-murder, Bill Diggs, "I have to kill him."

"Whoa, slow down. You're not killing anyone right here in the middle of town," Gabe said, as he turned to face Lucas.

Avigail calmly interjected, "Lucas, Eliza said you needed the banker alive to get access to all of the encrypted information you have on his client list. And,

Francisco is her father too. You might want to discuss it with her before killing him."

"You don't understand, I read through his account ledger in Monte Carlo. He took a ten-million euro payment from Farouk Kateb eleven years ago, right after Eliza was abducted." Then a hint of anger crawled across his face, "And for a solid year after that day, he made me feel like it was my fault she was taken. I'm killing that son-of-a-bitch!"

His earpiece crackled to life and Diggs spoke to him, "Lucas, don't move. Francisco isn't the only one here."

39

Lucas couldn't contain himself now. He came to his feet and turned, scanning for Francisco among the crowd of people on the walkway. Then he saw him, standing at the top of the marble steps leading up to the Royal Ingstedt Bank.

It took a minute to sink in. Francisco didn't look the same, but Lucas was only seventeen that last time he saw him. He looked weathered and hardened, like a man who didn't have a shred of joy in his life. Like a man of meager worth, wrapped in a ten-thousand euro Gieves & Hawkes tailored suit. A man trying to convince himself that he had everything, when in truth, he had nothing.

Lucas starting walking toward him, weaving slowly through the tourists that filled the sidewalk. He reached back and tapped the grip of his H&K .45

beneath the loose tail of his shirt to confirm its exact position on his hip. He was in total tunnel vision now, locked onto his prey and beginning the natural progression of killing intent.

His subconscious detected the rhythm of Francisco's chest rising and falling beneath the suit, and Lucas' breathing went into perfect synchronicity. When Francisco looked up, Lucas paused and looked away. It was the predator's dance of death.

Gabe stood up to follow him and turned to Avigail, "This is about to go bad in a big way. Be ready."

Diggs spoke into Lucas' earpiece again, "Lucas, the banker isn't alone. He has an armed escort. Two lengths behind him, gray suit and sunglasses. I can't detect any earpiece or communications, so he's probably solo. If you listen to me, we can still take him without getting killed."

Lucas paused on the sidewalk but remained fixated on his target.

"Good. Now turn around and walk back to Avigail, and try not to draw his attention."

Lucas turned and did as he was instructed.

Diggs talked him back to her side, "Excellent. Now listen. Francisco used to work with Avigail. She was a trusted confidante of the old Banco Baudin president, and deeply imbedded with Farouk Kateb. He knows her, and if Aziz did his job like a good little terrorist, he would have reported to his handlers in

Beirut that she had reappeared in Morocco. No one working with Hezbollah keeps secrets like that. So, it's plausible that Francisco already knows she might be here, since he is taking orders from the same people. Are you reading me?"

Lucas took a deep breath and let his heart return to its normal pace. He looked into Avigail's eyes as he was listening to Diggs, "Yes. I read you."

"Good. If Avigail approaches him first and acts like she is not surprised to see him, it might keep him calm. And calm is exactly how we want him right now. She can tell him that she is working for Aziz now, that she knew him very well because Farouk trained him, and he requested that she accompany him on this trip."

"Diggs, the plan is blown now. I can't go into the bank and pretend to be the emissary."

"I know that. But with Avigail's help, we might be able to get Francisco to come to us."

Lucas kept looking into Avi's soft green eyes, "Diggs, I won't put her in danger. She's already been hurt by Aziz."

The deeply imbedded earpieces that Diggs and Lucas were using picked up vibrations from the shell-shaped cochlea in the inner ear and converted them into sound when they spoke, so the person on the other end could only hear what they said, and no ambient noises or other people standing close.

Avigail, unable to hear the conversation going on

between Lucas and the man talking in his ear, tilted her head with a puzzled look, "Are you talking about me?" Then she seemed to realize that she had another role to play, "Whatever it is, I'll do it."

Lucas hesitated to let him know that Avigail was willing. "What do you want her to do?"

"Tell her to walk up to Francisco and greet him like she was expecting to see him, and tell him that Aziz is afraid to go into the bank. She can say he is paranoid that Interpol is looking for him, and he is worried the bank might have facial recognition scanners that would pick him out.

Francisco will likely not be surprised to hear that a young Hezbollah recruit is paranoid," Diggs said. "Then, she can say that he sent her to bring him to the marina, where he is waiting on a private boat."

Lucas relaxed a little more, "And I'll be waiting on the boat," he said.

"Yes. It's still going to be ugly when he recognizes you, but at least by then I can move into a following position and have a chance to take out the guard. With the guard gone, you, me, and Gabe can handle Francisco. We'll get him on the motor launch where Aziz is already waiting, and get them both back to the yacht as fast as possible."

40

Francisco saw her approaching from halfway down the block. She was hard to miss, even in a meandering crowd, a stunner in a red dress, waves of glimmering black curls that seemed to flow over and around her body. And the way she moved, with an athletic feline elegance was unlike anyone else. He had watched her moving through the office in Monte Carlo many times in years past, and it was a sight that few men could wipe from their mind.

As predicted by Diggs, he didn't seem entirely surprised that she was here.

She walked directly up to him, removed her sunglasses and smiled confidently, "Hello, Francisco."

"Avigail, I was told you might be accompanying Aziz Harrak. I was very pleasantly surprised to hear that you survived the disaster aboard Farouk's yacht in the Mediterranean. You'll have to tell me about it sometime."

"It's something I'd rather not relive, Francisco."

He looked at her carefully, not admiringly, as most men look at her, but thoughtfully. As if he was trying to appraise her, to set a value on her trustworthiness.

"Speaking of Aziz, where is he?"

"He sent me to find you. He has some concerns about being in public places with all the cameras and such. You know, Aziz hasn't traveled much, and he thinks the entire world is looking for him."

Francisco continued to study her, neither amused nor concerned by her explanation about the missing emissary, just assessing. "Will he be coming soon?"

"No. He would like for you to join him at the marina. He is waiting on a comfortable boat, and the privacy is more to his liking. He said he can discuss the account transfers with you there, then you can make them at your earliest convenience."

"That wasn't what I was told by our employers," Francisco said.

Avigail had known Francisco for many years, she had seen him interacting with her old boss, Berger, and also with some of the Middle Eastern clients who came to the office, the same men he now worked for directly. She knew he had a tendency to fold under duress, "I'm just delivering his request, Francisco. If you aren't happy with it, you should call the man in Beirut for instructions."

She knew Francisco would never do that. It would make him look weak and indecisive to people who wouldn't tolerate that from him. He was backed into a corner, either acquiesce and follow her to the marina or paint himself out to be a weakling to his superiors.

"Alright. Take me to him," he said.

She smiled, and put her glasses back on, and turned to walk across the street to the main pier of the marina. He looked to his left at the thick chested man in the gray suit standing a few yards away and motioned for him to follow.

Three quarters of the way down the long pier, Francisco saw the motor launch tied to a slot on the left side, and beneath the awning that stretched out over the sun deck, a man with tanned skin and black hair sat with his back to the pier, looking out over the water and the seagulls that were dancing in the air.

Avigail stopped before reaching the boat and gestured for Francisco to proceed alone. He approached the ramp to the boat, "Hello Aziz, I am finally pleased to meet you."

The man stood up and turned to face him. Francisco looked into the man's face, and though he hadn't met Aziz, the man was distinctly familiar. He had a chiseled, battle-hardened look, like he had spent years at war in the deserts of North Africa and the Mediterranean, which is exactly what Francisco expected. But something about him was incredibly and intimately familiar.

"Not who you were expecting?" Lucas said.

Francisco looked even more confused, the voice was familiar too. It sounded like … then the blood visibly drained from his handsome face, his shoulders tensed, and legs stiffened.

Francisco's guard picked up on the change, and he reached under his arm for a compact machine gun tucked away in a shoulder holster, but as he reached, the butt of a Glock pistol came crashing down on the back of his head and sent him sprawling across the wooden planks of the pier. Francisco wheeled around to see his guard out cold, and Bill Diggs standing over him. Diggs tucked the pistol away to keep from drawing more attention than necessary.

Francisco turned back to face his son, "You shouldn't be here, Lucas. In fact, you shouldn't be alive."

Lucas stepped onto the ramp to face him. Then a voice called out from down the pier, "Papa?"

IN THE MOMENTS of confusion and indecision when Lucas' father, Francisco, reemerged from the dead, no one had noticed Eliza arriving on the landing.

Tired of being confined to the yacht for over a week, and worried about what dangers her brother might be walking into, she had decided to come to Willemstad in the second shore boat.

Having shed the bonds of her traditional Muslim coverage, she looked radiant as she stood on the boardwalk in a shimmering lavender dress, and her long golden hair set loose in the breeze. She looked as if she'd been freed from her life of servitude and was returning to the world.

One of her personal guards, Mohammed, had driven her to town on the boat, and he was occupied trying to find a day-slip to store it. Normally he would have never left her side.

Francisco turned around and saw her; the little girl, who was no longer as he'd remembered her. The cold demeanor he had with Lucas crumbled when he realized who this woman really was. "Eliza?"

She smiled and nodded her head, and for an instant, she felt like a little girl again herself. She wanted to run to him and leap into his arms, but something held her back.

As the two of them were frozen in a father-daughter stare; Lucas was also frozen at the shock of his sister turning up in the middle of a very bad situation.

Diggs had the presence of mind to step forward with a small multi-tool and cut the wire band that secured the attaché case to Francisco's wrist. He snatched the case from his grip and stepped back.

Francisco came instantly back to the present. He looked at Diggs, then surveyed the surroundings with Lucas and Eliza. He had only one way out of this, and that was back down the long pier to the roadway. He turned back to face Lucas and without a moment's hesitation, he drew a 9mm Walther pistol from his trouser pocket and took aim at his chest.

LUCAS' childhood flashed in rapid sequences before his eyes. Moments of laughter, playing in the sea with his baby sister, his mother singing in the early mornings. He saw visions of his father, coming and going in the house, and mixing drinks at the bar.

Then, the visions stopped.

There was a flash of brilliant amber light. A high-pitched ringing in his ears, and the sudden sensation of weight on his chest, as if an anvil had fallen on him while he was peacefully sleeping. Then he felt like he was falling, a long weightless drop through the air, and it ended in a cushion of water.

He could feel the cool water, and the smell of salty brine encasing him and forcing him downward. The last thing he saw was the celeste blue of the sky, drifting further away through the green lens of the sea.

After shooting his son in the chest at point blank range, Francisco spun quickly and fired at Diggs, but he pulled up the attaché case and deflected the shot. He reached for his Glock, but before he could get to it, Francisco rushed into him and Diggs tripped over the prostrate body of the guard and fell backward onto the pier.

Eliza was frozen in shock, unable to reconcile in her mind what she had just witnessed. Her father was on her in a second, his arm wrapped around her neck and the Walther buried against her temple.

As Diggs got to his feet, Francisco was moving back down the pier, dragging Eliza and using her as a shield. Diggs trained the front sight of his gun on Francisco's head, but it was a small moving target, and too close to Eliza to risk a shot.

He turned to see if there was any sign of Lucas, just as Avigail dove into the water after him. He had to make a choice … he threw his pistol down into the boat and went into the water after Avigail.

Francisco dragged Eliza up to the edge of the roadway and let go of her neck, wrapping his arm around her waist instead, "Do exactly as I tell you, Honey, and we'll make it through this."

"That's far enough!" a voice yelled from behind.

Francisco turned to see Gabe, with a pistol drawn, standing on the walkway. He raised the Walther and began rapid firing in his direction. Pandemonium erupted on the street.

A pretty, middle-aged woman standing ten feet behind Gabe, collapsed on the street and was instantly laying in a growing puddle of blood. Gabe squatted and bolted to the left to get behind a trash can for cover, but with Eliza standing close, he couldn't return fire.

Eliza jerked and struggled until she broke free from her father's grasp, then Francisco turned and ran into the crowd. He vanished in seconds.

ELIZA AND GABE both came running down the pier and arrived at the boat just as Avigail and Diggs were pulling Lucas from the water up onto the diving deck of the boat. He appeared lifeless, no movement, no breathing.

Diggs rolled him over onto his stomach, reached under him and pulled his midsection up to let the water drain from his lungs. Then he rolled him onto his back again. "There's no blood. He must have worn his vest!" he said. He ripped open Lucas' shirt, and revealed the thin white body armor, with a single puncture in the center. He loosened the Velcro straps, and pulled it off.

Then Diggs held two fingers against Lucas' neck, "He doesn't have a pulse."

Diggs started a series of compressions on his chest with clasped palms, and after the twentieth, Avigail cradled Lucas' head and wrapped her lips over his, blowing air deeply into his lungs, three times.

Diggs checked for a pulse again, "Still nothing!"

He went back to forceful compressions, "Stay with me Lucas, Fight!"

The tears were beginning to stream down Avigail's cheeks as she leaned over a second time to force air into his lungs, and as she finished the last powerful breath, she felt his body shudder beneath her.

41

Lucas' senses were fully restored now. His chest hurt like hell, and he thought there might be a rib cracked where the bullet impacted his Spectra Shield vest, but he was alive. Alive, thanks almost entirely to her. If Avigail had hesitated for even a millisecond before coming into the water after him, he would have likely sunk to his death, as he was unconscious and sucking water into his lungs from the first instant.

She was sitting next to him on the rear lounge as the motor launch raced back to the safety of the yacht, anchored a few miles farther offshore. Gabe was at the wheel and Diggs was sitting opposite him, scanning the sea ahead with the attaché case in his lap. Twenty yards to their left, the other boat was keeping pace, with Eliza and Mohammed at the wheel.

Lucas glanced over at Avigail and thought how beautiful she looked. Her hair was tied back again, a few long strands were flitting around her face as the wind rushed past, and her long tanned legs were stretched forward on the teakwood deck. She let her head lean back against the cushion and rolled her eyes to the left, she smiled and stared into his eyes.

He was utterly captured by her. His entire adult life, he had devoted himself to war and killing, and deliberately avoided the temptations of women. But here in this place, in this one brief moment of pause from the evils that surrounded them, he knew that he loved this woman. In the time that had passed since he last saw her, she had never left his mind.

"You saved my life. It might take a long time for me to pay back that large a debt," he said.

"I didn't do it because I wanted you to owe me anything. I just did it … I did it because you are the only thing in my life that matters, and I can't lose you again."

She reached over and touched his forearm, then let her hand glide down over the artwork of Legionnaire tattoos and watchwords of honor etched in his skin. She clasped his hand in hers, and the warmth of it sent a wave washing through him.

Her hand was soft and delicate, like the petals of a flower wrapped around his hulking paw. Years of war and life in the desert heat, using his hands as tools and weapons, had strengthened and distorted them. The skin was dark and dry and calloused. Hands that should never be used to touch the smooth flesh of a woman.

THE BOATS REACHED THE YACHT, and Gabe and Mohammed hauled Aziz out from below the deck and carried him to a holding box near the engine room, as Lucas, Avigail, Diggs, and Eliza went to the main salon to plan their next move.

Diggs knew from the satellite surveillance photos that the girls were now being held in a house on the shore, not far from Bram Bay where the opium was delivered this morning. From the conversation Avigail heard between Aziz and the Cuban, they were being prepared there, and Raphael would deliver them tomorrow.

"We shouldn't wait for tomorrow," Diggs said. We have no idea where Francisco is, or if he is trying to make contact to warn them. If we want even a shred of hope to save those girls, we need to hit the house as fast as we can." He looked at Lucas for a response.

"Yes, I'm in. I can contact Serge, and have him meet us with weapons and tactical gear here," he said, pointing to a location on the satellite photo. "But do you have any idea what we're facing? Civilian guards? Cuban Special Forces, what?"

"My guess is, they are Cuban military, or part of the Cuban DI. The man leading this group, the one

Avigail saw this morning, is one of the best intelligence officers they have, Raphael Ortega. He's a ruthless bastard, and he leaves a trail of bodies everywhere he goes."

"I can come," Gabe said from behind. "This is one fight that Eli wouldn't mind me jumping into."

"We'll need someone to take us in with the boat, and then be prepared to extract fast. That would help."

Eliza pulled Lucas to the side, "Lucas, we need to talk about what just happened. About our father."

"We will, and there's a lot more that I need to tell you. But for now, he has shown us all we need to know about who he really is," Lucas said. "Let's get these little girls back to their families, then we can talk about ours."

As THE SUN was taking its last breath on the western horizon, and the stars were rising in the east, Lucas and Diggs were stepping off the bow of the motor launch onto the crunchy shell beach of Curaçao. They were at a deserted point only two kilometers from the big blue house on the shore, where the girls were being held captive.

Serge, Lucas' faithful friend from the Legion, was waiting in the tree line and flashed a laser beam to signal his location.

By 10:00 pm, the three-man team was armed and

moving in on the perimeter of the house. With night vision optics, they could see two guards outside the iron gate, heavily armed, sitting across from each other behind a low stone wall. They didn't seem to be on the alert for any particular danger and were passing a pint of rum back and forth.

"I don't think Francisco has sent up any warning flags yet, or if he contacted his people in Beirut, they didn't see any need to tell the Cubans," Diggs whispered.

"I see two more close to the house, one on each side of the door. If we shoot the two at the gate, the others will be prepared before we get there," Serge said.

"I'll take out the gate guards, you two take the door guards," Lucas said. He disappeared into the dark before Diggs could respond.

LUCAS SPENT the next thirty minutes inching forward in the darkness, closing the gap between himself and his next victims. Every time the two men spoke, or quarreled over the rum, or farted and laughed, he moved closer. Soon he found himself lying flat against the outside of the stone wall, only a few feet away. He had a ten-inch, Spanish Belduque blade in his right hand.

They were definitely Cuban military. He could understand their Spanish, but they used slang that was typical of the Caribbean islands. Then one of them made a fatal mistake. He lit a cigar.

Lucas heard the match strike, and he saw the bright glow of the flame and the pulsing of the match and tobacco. The sudden flash of the light shocked the guards' pupils and caused a moment of night-blindness.

Lucas flew over the wall like a ghost, and as his feet hit the dirt his blade was plunging through the neck of the guard on the right, cutting through arteries, cartilage and tissue. Then he pulled it back and spun around, slashing into the darkness where he instinctively knew the other man's neck would be. He felt the steel slice through flesh and bone, nearly decapitating him. Lucas took a half step back, as the two men both collapsed forward on top of each other.

SERGE MANAGED to climb into a tree for a better vantage. He flipped on the night vision scope of his lightweight Steyr rifle and found the two door-guards in the green shadows. He could see Diggs moving along the edge of the house and approaching the front corner, where a guard was standing only two feet on the other side. Serge squeezed off a silenced shot.

From Diggs position, he couldn't hear the little rifle fire, but the soft sizzle of the .223 caliber bullet boiling through the moist air was a distinctive sound that you don't forget. And the impact on a man's skull only feet away from you was another. One second later, another shot came from the darkness and dropped the other guard before he knew his companion was already dead.

Lucas and Diggs went in through the front door. Lucas crouched low, so Diggs had a line of fire over his left shoulder. Lucas moved right, sweeping the H&K pistol through his field of vision, and Diggs went left. The lights were on, but the house was silent.

Then they heard footsteps upstairs. Someone moving swiftly, in short strides. Now they were coming down the stairs quickly. Both men pulled their aim to the staircase, just as the housekeeper, Diana appeared.

When she saw the two men with guns aiming at her, she froze, and her short arms reached for the sky. Lucas raised one finger to his lips, "*Silencio*…" She nodded that she understood and wasn't going to make a sound. He kept the gun on her and moved close enough to whisper, "Who else is in the house?"

She shook her head.

"No one else? If you lie to me, I will kill you," he said.

"Nadie, Señor!" (No one!) "Only the girls."

Lucas looked over at Diggs, then back at Diana, "You're telling me the truth?"

"Si Señor. They are all upstairs."

Serge peered in through the front door, rifle barrel first, then stepped in behind them.

Lucas motioned for him to hold the housekeeper under gun while they went upstairs to sweep for other guards, and check for the girls.

As they moved from room to room on the second floor, they found the same thing. Two young girls in each of the first bedrooms, drugged into a sleepy state, and only partially clothed. In the third bedroom, there was only one girl, five in all. Lucas pulled out the sat phone and called Gabe, who was waiting with the motor launch a quarter mile off the beach.

Diggs went downstairs and confronted the housekeeper, "There were seven girls, where are the other two?" he said with a menacing stare.

"These are all they brought here; they are supposed to leave tomorrow. But they told me one died before they brought them here."

"I'm looking for the one called Camila. Which one is Camila?"

"Oh! Camila came many days ago with Señor Raphael. She left this morning before the sunrise on the fast boat. I don't know where they were taking her, they don't tell me such things."

"What about Raphael, where is he?"

"He left on a small plane today. I believe they said he was going back to Cuba."

Diggs turned away and cursed under his breath. Camila was the one he desperately wanted. Not to liberate her, but to use her as leverage. He didn't care what deals Mathew Penn might have made with Esteban Aguera.

Diggs knew he was responsible for the death of Mariella Martinez. He was going to kill Esteban, and he thought having Camila would give him an edge. But Camila it seemed, was already gone.

42

The Signal Intelligence (SIGINT) facility in the jungles of Lourdes, Cuba, is the home base of mother Russia's spying and intelligence gathering service against the United States. Raphael had arrived at a small dirt landing strip at midday in a Cessna 180, and he was glued to the satellite monitors, watching the steady progression of the speed boat loaded with Venezuelan gold.

Several times the boat had slowed, then resumed its steady cruising speed of forty-three knots, but the Caribbean is unpredictable. There are rogue waves, sudden squalls over patches of warm water and reefs, and many other things that might have caused the boat to slow down, and then resume speed. But it never fully stopped, and never diverted from its steady course to the southern edge of Cuba. It appeared

Antonio would arrive at Camp Matanzas as projected.

After seventeen hours of droning vibrations from the roaring engines, the motion of the hull rolling up and down the waves, and occasionally banging on the water so hard it could snap your teeth, Camila was violently ill.

Three times, Antonio had to slow the boat down so she could escape from the cabin and hang over the gunwale to vomit into the sea. He wasn't the fatherly type, he'd never been around children, but he tried to comfort her. He held her hair away from her face as she puked, and wiped her cheeks and forehead with a cool damp rag after she was done. Then he would help her back to the cabin and lay her on the bed before resuming his duties at the wheel and throttles.

He gave her a heavy dose of Dramamine after the last episode, and she fell into a deep sleep. She wouldn't wake up again until they were almost there.

The Tirranna entered Cuban territorial waters, twelve miles from the southern tip of the island, seven minutes earlier than the original Garmin projections on the computer. Antonio had made up some time after his last slowdown.

"Do you think the Cubans saw you slow down?" Mathew said.

"I'm sure they see everything. But I've had to slow

down many times for a patch of rough water, or for the girl to throw up, so it would have looked normal. Don't worry, I'm a professional," Antonio answered.

THE LAST SLOWDOWN Antonio made was four miles off the coast of Haiti, passing close enough to see the lights of Port-au-Prince. As he slowed, another boat came alongside, and a passenger jumped aboard, Mathew Penn.

In his years of service, hunting, mingling, and watching the rock star lives of cartel bosses and corrupt political enemies of the United States, the CIA Station Chief of Caracas had come to one conclusion, crime pays.

Mathew was tired. Tired of the bullshit orders from fashion-tie wearing assholes in Washington. Tired of living in a crap apartment in a neighborhood that smelled like human piss and month-old garbage. And it was never going to end. He knew that nothing he could do in his career would make any real difference in the world, and no difference in his future.

When he saw Diggs come into the CIA cave in the US Embassy, a man he used to worship and envy, he knew it was all for nothing. Diggs had spent forty years doing it, but now what did he have? A broken down shack in Winchester, Virginia, a pension that wasn't enough to repair the roof, and he was utterly alone in the world.

When Esteban approached him with the details of Raphael's plans to transfer the gold and Camila to Cuba using Antonio, Mathew made him an offer he couldn't refuse. Full asylum and citizenship in the states for himself and Camila, and Mathew takes the gold.

Esteban didn't really care about the gold, because he had many times that amount of cash safely tucked away in banks in Panama, Barbados and Bimini. He even had an account at the private Investors Division of Citibank in New York City. All he needed was to be free to live in America and leave the cartel life of Venezuela. He might even make some extra money consulting for the DEA and the CIA.

Esteban would help Mathew offload the gold to a secured warehouse in Miami and slowly convert it to invested cash. Mathew would put in for retirement at the end of the next year and come home to a life of wealth and women.

The phone calls on office lines that he knew were recorded, the meeting between Esteban, Mathew, and Diggs, they were all part of the ruse. But Mathew knew better than to trust anyone, so he demanded to join Antonio somewhere in the voyage and be there with his gold when it landed on US soil. If they were intercepted somewhere along the way by American authorities, he'd flash his CIA Station

Chief badge and tell them he was on official business.

As Antonio and Mathew entered Cuban waters, they could see the occasional lights of small villages along the coast, but they didn't dare run too close in the dark, as there are razor sharp coral reefs that would carve the boat out from under them in a second. But they needed to maintain the illusion that they were following as close to the island as possible, until just before they reached the point at Camp Matanzas.

The sea was beginning to turn to chop in the last few miles before they came to the territorial waters. Antonio looked to the east, and couldn't see stars any longer, only pitch black skies, "There's weather moving in from the east, maybe a storm. But it's still far out."

"Is that going to slow us down when we make a break?"

"No. This boat can run at full speed through much rougher water. It will help us, because the old tubs the Cubans use for patrol boats on the boundary won't stand a chance. They won't even come after us in rough seas."

They had to go almost to the turn-in to Camp Matanzas before they reached the GPS point that was the shortest distance to US territorial waters. Once they made the break, which would be instantly recognized by the people watching them on satellite feeds, they would have to run at full throttle for ninety-two minutes to reach the safety of the Florida Keys. After that, Antonio had perfected routes that blended with normal boating traffic that would take them all the way to Miami.

Antonio was at the helm, throttles in his right hand, and tapping the GPS screen with his left. Mathew was strapped into the cushioned racing seat next to him, watching the dark horizon. "We are almost there ...," Antonio said. He looked up from the screens, "There, at eleven o'clock, two patrol boats! This is where we say goodbye!"

He simultaneously thrust the throttles fully up and wheeled the boat forty-five degrees to starboard. As the engines howled and the big boat made a sharp turn to the right, young Camila was thrown from the bed in the cabin below and slammed against the hull. She groaned as her head struck the fiberglass and was immediately unconscious again.

Antonio found his new course heading in three seconds, locked the auto-pilot on direction, then shut down all of the boats exterior and cockpit lighting to go into full dark-running mode. It was something he had done a hundred times over.

Mathew was startled by the sudden rush of speed and the violence of the boat ricocheting across the waves at over sixty miles per hour. He had to scream at the top of his lungs to be heard, "Are you sure the boat can take this?"

Antonio laughed, and trimmed out the engines another half degree, which picked the speed up another two miles per hour. Then he threw his head back and yelled, "Waaahooo!"

43

As they lifted the last young girl onto the deck of the yacht, Mohammed came out and took her in his arms, "The Sultana has cabins for the girls, and she is caring for them. She asks if you know how we might contact their parents to let them know they are safe?"

Diggs answered, "I'll call my contacts at the Embassy in Caracas as soon as I make another call first."

With Lucas standing at his side, Diggs' first phone call was to Eli Moskarov, "Eli, any word on Francisco Martell?"

"We have video of him leaving the first flight off the island after your run-in, which was a seaplane hop to Tortuga. After that, he vanished. He's in the wind now, my friend. Better to sit back and wait to catch him at one of his cash reserves. I'm sure he has several around the Caribbean."

"We have encrypted files he left behind and a flash drive of his former clients, but it's been impossible for us to crack it. We need someone really talented to handle it for us."

"I assume you've been introduced to the young lady working for Mathew Penn at the Embassy, Beth Michaelson?"

"Yes, his new analyst."

"He is wasting her as an analyst. I tried to recruit her out of MIT long before the CIA knew who she was. She might be the most gifted cryptographer I've ever seen. She's a genius at breaking digital coding and encryption, but she had some serious moral reservations about doing that kind of work for any government. Guess it's a millennial thing."

"I'll talk to her. My next phone call is the embassy anyway."

"Bill, there's something else. We have satellite photos of a big racing style boat leaving the dock at the house you just raided, before the sun came up. We've been tracking it every ninety minutes when our bird passes over, and it was on a direct course to Cuba."

"That wouldn't surprise me. The housemaid told us about a boat leaving early, with a girl on board, and Raphael Ortega flew out earlier for Cuba."

"Well, that boat just made a breakaway and is

running for the Florida Keys, at a very high rate of speed. The interesting thing is, there were four Cuban patrols within a quarter mile of him, and they didn't make a move."

"They let him run without a chase?"

"Not even a shot across the bow. I think someone gave them the orders to stand down and let him go."

Diggs was trying to process what Raphael could possibly have loaded on that boat, besides Camila Aguera, that he would want to send to the United States by way of a fast mule-boat. He couldn't come up with any immediate answers. "Eli, can you update me every hour and half when your satellite passes over? I have one more call to make, then Lucas and I are taking the new company jet for a trip to Florida."

"No problem. Talk to you soon."

"Eliza, Diggs just talked to the US Embassy in Caracas. An envoy is going to contact all of the parents of these girls and arrange for them to be flown to Willemstad tomorrow morning. If you can keep the girls safe, and have Gabe take them into the city in the morning; their parents will be waiting for them at the pier. They won't ask any questions, and Gabe won't offer any answers."

"What are you and Bill going to do?" Eliza asked.

"We are going to the island now to take the jet.

Diggs thinks there might be something more urgent about to happen, and we need to be there."

"What about ... father?"

"The Mossad said he flew off the island quickly and disappeared. But we have the encrypted files in his briefcase and the data on the flash drive. Diggs spoke to a girl at the CIA in Caracas who can probably help us crack the data, and we might be able to hunt him down. I promise we'll talk about it as soon as this is over."

"Will this ever be over, Lucas?"

He put his arms around her and pulled her close, "One day it will, I promise. But we both knew going into this, that there are a lot of evil men out there who need to die. And if we don't do it, who will?"

"Is our father one of them now, Lucas? Are we going to have to kill him?" she said. Then she put her face down into her hands to shield the tears.

"I don't know Eliza. I don't know."

44

Raphael was surrounded by a company of Russian SVR officers and Cuban Intelligence operatives. They were watching a live satellite feed of the Tirranna as it suddenly broke course and accelerated in a north-west trajectory.

Raphael smiled.

"Comrade Ortega, they are running away!" one of the young Cuban agents said.

A young Russian operator chimed in, "Sir, we have an armed drone on the runway. We can launch and sink them before they reach the protection of the United States territory."

"No. Let them be on their way," said the tall Russian standing behind Raphael.

~

Raphael Ortega was no one's fool. Even though he had Esteban's daughter, he kept an eye on the old military cartel commander. He knew his connections with the mule, Antonio, ran deep, and his spies had photographed the CIA Station Chief along with another man visiting Esteban's private estancia. He suspected a double-cross could be at hand, so he made a contingency.

One of the crates stored in the hull of Antonio's boat was actually loaded with 150 lbs of Semtex, with a satellite operated remote trigger supplied by his Russian comrade. And just for good measure, another crate contained a sealed bladder with 200 lbs of depleted nuclear reactor fuel, uranium-234, obtained from a sympathetic Argentinian official who oversees the disposal of nuclear waste from that country's three active nuclear power plants.

The fifty-nine foot Tirranna was a sea-delivered dirty bomb that, if for example, was parked in the inland water channel to downtown Miami on a Saturday morning, old Thunder Boat Row, would cause the most American civilian casualties of any foreign attack in history.

The explosion and resulting shockwave would level three square blocks of waterfront commercial property, killing five-thousand people instantly. The nuclear waste material, vaporized into a fine mist by the explosion and sent upward in a heat-ball to the lower atmosphere, would then be distributed by the prevailing winds over fifty square miles of the most densely populated area of the Sunshine State.

The final death toll would rack up in agonizingly slow form. First, with tens of thousands of cases of radiation poisoning, and later with hundreds of thousands of unexplained varieties of cancers. Parts of the Miami-Dade County metro area would be uninhabitable for ten generations.

The nuclear materials would be traced back to their Argentinian roots, and the Semtex chemical tags would lead back to the old Czech Republic, but the Americans wouldn't know who to blame or attack in retaliation.

45

Antonio could see distant thunderheads rolling in the direction of the Bahamas, the normally green coastal waters were flushed gray as the storm surge was slowly building. They followed the shoreline, then turned into the Miami River. They motored slowly now, encircled by towering skyscrapers and condos as they passed Brickell Key and entered the Miami River Greenway.

Raphael leaned forward to get a closer look at the grainy image on the monitor. He could make out the basic shape of the Tirranna, and three human heat signatures.

"Sweet little Camila, she could have been an excellent operative with a few more years of training."

The Russian was standing and watching over his shoulder, "It's a shame about the gold. But it's a very small price to pay for the glorious victory we are going to have over the corrupt Americans."

Raphael knew the Castros would be pissed-off about losing the gold, but he didn't give a shit about the money at this moment. He was elated. He was finally about to realize his most beautiful fantasy. To reap a terrible revenge on the people who spurned him as a child. The nation, the people of the very city where he was born, who had cast him out to struggle and starve in the streets of Havana. He was about to make them pay.

In truth, Raphael had known for some time now that Esteban and Mathew were planning to steal the gold and get Camila back at the same time. They were unimaginative, and not very careful in their communications. It was easy to discern what their plan really was.

He also knew from Esteban's old military files, that he had a sister in Miami who had once been linked romantically to Antonio, and that Antonio still regularly used a marine loading dock in the central waterway of Miami harbor. It was too easy to figure out their plan.

46

Diggs was looking out the window of the jet and talking on an encrypted telephone. He had relayed through several high-level communications channels to reach a National Reconnaissance Office outpost, in a nondescript building at the Naval Air Station on Key West.

"Can you see the boat on thermal image scans?"

"Yes, sir. We have the target in sight, and it's entering the Miami bay area now."

Diggs waited patiently for more details.

"Mr. Diggs, I'm picking up a recurring signal."

"Is it a transmitter signal from the boat? Are they tracking it?"

"No sir. This is a satellite ping. An incoming ping to a receiver that's located *on* the boat. And there's something else. It's coming from a Russian SVR bird."

Diggs turned to Lucas, "Holy shit, they've got the boat wired."

"Wired with what?" Lucas asked.

"It could be anything. Chemical, biological weapon, a suitcase sized one-kiloton nuclear device, who the hell knows. But the only reason the Russians and Cubans would have a boat wired to receive a signal directly from an SVR Satellite is because it's a bomb of some kind." He went back to the NRO operator at Key West, "Find a way to jam that signal, at all costs!"

THE G550 JET was cleared for special landing at a private defense contractor's landing strip, right on the edge of Miami Harbor. When Lucas, Diggs, and Serge came running off the plane, there was a Coast Guard swift boat waiting at the bulkhead, only one hundred yards away.

The instant they leapt aboard, the crewmen threw off the lines and the captain put full throttles to the armored speed boat. They had visual sightings of a boat that matched the description of the Tirranna just two miles from their location and heading directly up Miami River to downtown.

As the Coast Guard boat roared around Dodge Key, they could see the black Tirranna slowing up ahead and coming to a marina. Serge had pulled a handful of components out of his duffle bag and was rapidly assembling a menacing long-range weapon. His handmade Nemesis sniper rifle, chambered in .338 Lapua Magnum. He inserted and twisted the long heavy barrel and snapped a locking ring, then retracted the folding stock and pushed the scope down into its preset bases.

The Tirranna was idling to a stop now. Through the binoculars Diggs could see a man standing on the dock and waving. It was Esteban Aguera. The other more surprising person he saw was Mathew Penn in the boat, next to the driver. "Traitor." he muttered.

Camila was standing in the bow, waving at her father, when the Coast Guard captain hit the thundering sirens and flashing lights on the swift boat and hailed them, "Black Cigarette Boat, this is the U.S Coast Guard! Stop your engines and prepare to be boarded!"

Antonio's reaction was cat-like. He spun the Tirranna's helm like a roulette wheel and slammed the throttles home. All six engines screamed, and the boat violently rolled on her side, leaving a deep green whirlpool where the hull had been idling deep in the water only an instant before.

Camila was catapulted into the air and landed so hard in the water that the impact knocked the breath completely out of her. She was flailing and sinking at the same time. Her father, Esteban, stood helplessly on the dock, yelling at her, but he couldn't save her.

Esteban had spent his life living near the sea but never learned to swim.

"She's drowning!" Serge yelled at the Coast Guard captain. "Get me close and I'll save her!"

As the swift boat came close, Serge turned to Lucas, "The rifle is zeroed at four-hundred meters. Kill that son-of-a-bitch!" Then he dove off the side and swam to Camila, pulling her head up to the air just as she was going under.

The Coast Guard boat wheeled and went into fast pursuit of the Tirranna, but Antonio was gaining speed and pulling away. The two tons of gold in the hull was keeping him from reaching full speed, but at this rate, by the time they passed the last island before hitting the open ocean, Virginia Island, they would be more than eight-hundred meters ahead, over half a mile. The water was still fairly smooth in the protected bay, but once they hit the ocean the rough-water racing Tirranna would quickly become just a memory.

Lucas grabbed the long rifle and lay out over the bow of the boat and drew the bolt back on the Nemesis to chamber a cartridge. He reckoned the Tirranna was already over six-hundred meters ahead, so he would have to hold the scope two mil-dots high. With both boats racing over light waves at different rhythms, the riflescope reticle looked like a bouncing ball trying to settle on his target. It was going to be an impossible shot.

He sat upright and pulled the gun up over his knees, letting his upper body sway in contrast to the rhythm of the boat rolling over waves, and that settled it down a bit, but he was still going to need a lot of luck on his side just to hit any vital part of the big boat. He took two deep breaths, let half out, and squeezed the trigger.

The rifle barked and a second later a visible fireball came off the second-to-right engine cowling. Diggs was spotting through the binoculars, "Hit! Hold another mil high, and half-a-mil left for the wind!"

Lucas chambered another round and settled into his shooting rhythm again. Two breaths, hold, … squeeze.

As Diggs watched, the windshield in front of Antonio was splattered with red liquid, and the old King of Thunder Boat Row fell over the dashboard, then flopped to the deck. Mathew Penn turned around and looked at Diggs with a combination of astonishment and abject fear.

Then, he pulled Antonio's body to the side, stepped into his place and took the wheel. The throttles were still at full burn, with five engines racing when they passed Virginia Island and the ocean swells immediately rose in front of the Tirranna. But Penn had no other good options, this was his only chance to lose them.

He kept the black boat's nose into the wind and the engines going full blast and quickly pulled away from the Coast Guard swift boat, vanishing into the darkening waves.

~

Raphael was raging. Moments before his greatest triumph, his ultimate revenge on the American capitalists, a mysterious electromagnetic pulse had fried every circuit in the Russian SIGINT facility.

As he frantically pushed the detonation transmit button, nothing happened.

He sat staring at a completely dead, blank monitor.

"This isn't over," he said under his breath.

Mathew Penn had the gold. All of his dreams and most twisted desires lay beneath his feet in the belly of the big Tirranna. And unbeknownst to him, a highly radioactive bomb.

He was racing into the throat of a massive tropical storm, trying to make the Bahamas before running out of fuel. He charted the GPS for Grand Bahama and was trying his best to hold a straight course, but the seas were rolling in twenty-footers, and the boat was rising and crashing down the face of incoming waves. At best, he was getting twenty-five knots forward motion now.

The lightning strikes were blistering across the sky all around him, and the wind was driving the rain down in flesh-ripping sheets. He hunkered below the windscreen and shielded his face with one hand, while trying to steer with the other. Then, he felt something shift, and the boat quivered.

Two of the straps that were locking down the crates of gold had broken loose in the violent torment, and two-thousand pounds of weight was beginning to shift and slide with the movement of the sea. He kept the throttles up, and struggled to keep a heading, but the boat started to pitch and yaw, ignoring his commands through the steering wheel.

He was coming up the face of a towering wave when the boat suddenly flung herself sideways into the air as it crested the top. The Tirranna flipped in the whirling spray, the engines over-revved wildly when the propellers came out of the water, and the boat's electrical system began to fault. Fuses and wiring coils below deck blew and sparked, and fire erupted in the fuel cells just as she crashed into the following wave and plunged below the water.

The Semtex went off as the Tirranna was buried by the waves. The explosion expanded into an enormous chamber under the water, then raised the surface in a boiling rage like a depth-charge. The boat, the gold, the radioactive materials, and Mathew Penn, were all scattered into fragments and sent to the depths of the Atlantic trench.

47

ONE WEEK LATER - SOMEWHERE NEAR ST. MARTINIQUE IN THE CARIBBEAN

Lucas came awake, but he kept his eyes closed. He wanted to enjoy the feeling. The warmth of Avi's flesh pressed against him, entangled around him, as she continued to sleep. He could smell the lemongrass oil in her glistening black hair, and feel her slow, deep breath against his chest.

They made love last night. A powerful, visceral kind of love, born of danger and survival, and emotions that circumvented rational thought. Love that devours the senses and reaches into the soul. That was the nature of whatever this was that they had together. It wasn't explainable, but the love they felt for each other couldn't be denied.

He felt her stir, and she sighed as she came up from the dream. She didn't want it to end either. He tightened his arm around her, and she touched his cheek, "Can't we stay here forever?"

"Not forever, but for a while longer."

WHEN LUCAS CAME up to the main salon level of the yacht and out onto the rear deck, Eliza was already sitting in the morning sun and eating breakfast. He joined her, and sat without speaking for a time, just sipping coffee and watching the green sea around them come to life.

Then he spoke, "Diggs received a communication from Eli Moskarov last night. It seems a facial scanner picked up Francisco yesterday walking through the airport in New York."

"What are you going to do when you find him?"

"The same thing I'm going to do to everyone else on the list. I'm going to kill him. He showed us very clearly that he isn't our father anymore, that he's a part of that world that both of us have sworn to bring down. He demonstrated that when he shot me in the chest without so much as blinking an eye."

She knew he was right. The father she remembered, the one she thought had always loved and cherished her, who she dreamed had spent his final years searching in vain for her, was only a man she remembered through a little girl's eyes. The man she saw on the pier in Curaçao was a monster.

Lucas spoke again, "I've been thinking about something else too. You don't have to stay in this life anymore, Eliza. This life with the Sultan of Maladh.

You can leave. You can get away cleanly from him, and if he tries to come after you, I'll kill him just like all the others. He's a slaver, Eliza. He kidnapped you away from me when you were only eleven years old."

"Hassan was just a boy when they took me, Lucas. And he's always been kind to me. But I won't stay in this life forever. I promise I'll come home soon."

"How are you going to explain what's happened during the last two weeks? Your guards, the yacht crew, they'll talk. He's going to demand answers from you."

"He might, but I can handle him. Trust me. I'll leave when I'm ready. When we have enough resources to finish this war we've started. And when I'm ready to leave, no one will stand in my way."

"And if he tries?"

"It might sound strange, but in many ways I love Hassan. But if he tries to keep me from leaving when I decide it's time for me to go, then I'll kill him myself."

Diggs came onto the deck, "Beth Michaelson has been working with the digital files and the encrypted data on the flash drive and making some progress. She wants to join us, to be part of the Fairhope Group."

"She's willing to leave the CIA?" Eliza said.

"She knows we're doing something that's outside the boundaries of normal, and she likes it."

"If she can dig out enough information from Francisco's files to help sort out where he might be going, let's bring her in," Lucas said.

"She's already done it. We have a good idea where he's running to, or *who* he's running to. And, she's hacked the transitional account he set up at Royal Ingsted Bank. Guess how much you just inherited from your father?"

48

WEST PALM BEACH, FLORIDA USA

"I still think it's too early for you to start going to school again, Camila."

"I can't stop living, Aunt Marguerite. I want to go to school here in the United States and start making new friends. This is my home now, and father tells me I need to be strong and move on with my life," Camila said.

They were standing in the open kitchen of Marguerite Aguera's (Esteban's sister) home on the inlet of West Palm Beach, Florida. A lavish tropical French design, originally built by a Parisian fashion icon. Camila and her father were living with her until he completed a few of the "cooperation" assignments with the DEA that would guarantee approval of their permanent visas.

"Go upstairs to say goodbye to your father, then I will drive you to school," Marguerite said.

Esteban was in the upstairs study, speaking to someone on the telephone when Camila entered the room. He held the phone against his chest, "I'm on an important call, Camila, what do you need?"

"I'm leaving for school now."

"Good. It will be very healthy for you to start improving your English and getting used to life here. I will see you later this evening for dinner."

Camila stood staring at him a moment longer, hoping perhaps for an embrace or a kind word about how she looked in her new school uniform. But Esteban was not a man to show affection or empathy.

A sharp noise from downstairs startled Camila. She turned and called down the stairs for her aunt, "Aunt Marguerite, is everything alright?"

There was no response.

Esteban called to her, "Marguerite, did you break something? Answer me!" There was no response to his demand. He put the phone back to his ear, "I need to call you back in just a few minutes."

Esteban and Camila went down the spiraling oak stairs together and passed through the main living area. They called to Marguerite again, but again she didn't answer. Camila walked into the Kitchen and froze stiff as a board in the entryway. Esteban walked up behind her, and his face went instantly pale.

Marguerite's lifeless body lay spread across the kitchen island, her throat sliced through to the bone, blood dripping from the granite counter to a large spreading pool on the white tile floor. Both Camila and Esteban stood open-mouthed in disbelief. It was a cartoonish-horror display that couldn't be real. Then Camila looked to her left.

From behind the open door to the pantry stepped the dark-tanned Cuban they both knew so well, Raphael Ortega.

He still had the knife in his hand that had killed Marguerite. A long military-style bowie from the 1960s, like the old-school killers of the Bolivarian Revolution were known to carry. In his other hand, he held a Makarov .380 pistol, which he quickly raised and pointed directly at Esteban.

As he held the gun on Esteban, he looked at Camila and smiled, "Come to me, Camila. Please, come here and be with me."

She felt her body lean forward and take a step, without consciously wanting to. His voice held a power over her, a grip on her soul. Esteban grabbed her by the shoulders and held her in place.

"Let her go Esteban, or I'll end this quicker than you want." He called to her again, "Come on Camila, you know you want to be with me. I rescued you, and I love you more than anyone ever has."

Esteban let go of her, and she stumbled forward, dragging her new brown leather sandals through the pooling blood on the floor. She came to his side, and he smiled at her again, the same broad beaming smile that he had on his face just before he shot her chaperone Silvia, in the face. It was only a little more than a month past, but it felt like a lifetime. A hazy vague memory that had nearly been wiped away by now.

Raphael pulled her close and spun her to face her father, with his armed wrapped tightly around her body and the Makarov now pinned against her temple. She stood looking at Esteban with, oddly, not a trace of fear in her eyes. Nothing but a blank, emotionless stare.

"I told you what I was going to do if you didn't hold up your end of our agreement, Esteban," Raphael said. "Now you are going to watch your little girl die. Then I'm going to kill you."

"No! Please don't kill her, she hasn't done anything to deserve this!"

Raphael stood silently for a moment. Then responded, "I might be persuaded to let her live, if she will do one thing for me." Then he pulled her long hair to the side so he could look into her dark brown eyes, "You must kill your father, Camila."

Esteban looked gut-punched, but he didn't say a word.

"You know he never tried to rescue you, all that time you were held captive. He never wanted you to come back. He didn't even try to save you when you were drowning in front of his eyes. You want to kill him; you know you do."

Camila looked at him and felt the power of his

voice pulling at her again. It was true, he had freed her from the bonds and torment, only Raphael had cared enough to take her away from the misery, and she had thought many times that her father had given up on her.

"If you do this one thing, Camila, it will set you free from all of your troubles. I will take you to a wonderful place in the Caribbean islands, and you will have a beautiful life. You just need to do this one little thing to take that next step."

He reached around in front of her and held the long bowie in his open palm. She watched, as if from a distance away from her body, as her fingers grasped the leather handle and lifted it, feeling the weight of the heavy steel blade pulling down on her little-girl's arm. Raphael loosened his grip of her, she moved silently across the floor and stood in front of her father, with the long blade pointed towards his middle.

She was completely void of emotion, or maybe her soul had moved on to another place, away from the carnage that was about to happen. Esteban stared in disbelief, and tears were beginning to well in his eyes. He looked down at the blade, the tip pressed against his belly, and a teardrop fell from the end of his nose.

As it plopped on the flat side of the long knife, Camila startled awake from her dream. She looked at the knife, not remembering how it came to be in her hand, then she looked up into her father's eyes. She turned and looked pleadingly at Raphael, "I can't do this, please don't make me!"

Raphael looked disappointed, but he knew she hadn't been through enough conditioning yet, to expect such a big leap in control. "It's alright, come back to me."

She came back to his side, and as she did, Raphael raised the Makarov again and fired twice into Esteban's chest. He stumbled backward into the living area, and fell over a green French Provincial chair, then collapsed on the floor.

Raphael walked up calmly and stood over him as he gasped for air, while the blood began to gurgle up from his lungs. He stood there, enjoying his revenge for the longest time, then, he fired another shot to Esteban's forehead, just above the left eye.

Raphael walked back to the kitchen island, where Camila was standing. "I'm sorry. I don't ever want to disappoint you," she said. He stepped closer and smiled at her, then reached down and brushed the hair back over her ears.

Then he felt the piercing fire. A feeling of hot burning pain that reached under his ribs and up into his chest. He looked down and saw young Camila's hand wrapped around the leather handle, and the long blade buried deeply in his left side.

His legs buckled and he fell hard. He grimaced as his knees smashed into the floor. As he fell, Camila withdrew the blade. Now she stood over him, staring down into *his* confused eyes.

"That bastard never cared for me anyway. He treated my mother like trash until he killed her, and he sent me away to be raised by someone else. I know what he really was … he was a drug dealer and he kidnapped and sold girls just like me. He was no different than you, Raphael! But still, it's not nice to kill your own father. Thank you for doing it for me."

She reached back with the long blade and swung down across his neck. He groaned and fell onto his side and was silent an instant later.

CAMILA PLACED the blade on the kitchen counter and walked calmly upstairs to her bedroom. She drew a hot tub of water in her private bath, then undressed, being careful to lay out her school clothes neatly on the bed. As the tub was filling, she dampened a washcloth and dabbed away a few random spots of blood from her blouse.

Then she stepped gently into the tub of hot water and eased herself down to her neck.

"This can all be washed away," she said to herself. "Everything that's happened to me, can be washed away."

WHAT DID YOU THINK?

Thank you for reading ***Emissary of Vengeance***.

If you liked it, I have a favor to ask. Like all other authors these days, my success depends entirely on you. Your opinions and thoughts about the book are all that matter. People want to know what you think.

Please, take a minute and share your thoughts in a brief review. You can help make this book a success!

Just sign in to your Amazon account, go to the sales page for ***Emissary of Vengeance***, and click the button that says (**Write a Review**) near the bottom of the page.

THANK YOU!

ALSO BY WILLIAM JACK STEPHENS

~

Mallorca Vendetta

~

Emissary of Vengeance

~

Where The Green Star Falls

~

Andalusian Legacy

ABOUT THE AUTHOR

Jack has lived and explored the world from the Arctic to the southern reaches of Patagonia, and now splits his time between a home in the USA, and one in the Andes Mountains of southern Argentina.

In his former life, he served in executive roles with some of the largest companies in the world. He spear-headed investigations with government agents, gave private counseling to congressional leaders, and served on committees that planned for nuclear, biological, or chemical disaster.

Now he writes gripping thrillers, tales of adventure, and the occasional love story.

www.williamjackstephens.com

Emissary of Vengeance is a work of fiction. Names, characters, businesses, places, events and incidents are either the products of the author's imagination or used in a fictitious manner. Any resemblance to actual persons, living or dead, or actual events is purely coincidental.

ASIN: B0829BWJ9T

ISBN: 9781659647457

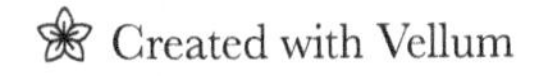